MR. HOTNESS

PEYTON BANKS

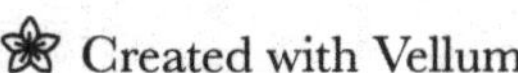 Created with Vellum

Mr. Hotness was previously featured in the Tangled Sheets anthology. This version has been expanded to include the ending! Enjoy!

Peyton Banks

"Mr. Hotness alert!" Alana Thornton whispered fiercely as she bolted from the couch in an attempt to run to the door. Her foot connected with the corner of the coffee table. "Ouch!"

Tiptoeing toward the door of the apartment, Sofie chuckled. "You're so damn clumsy."

Feminine giggling could be heard in the hallway, along with a deep, baritone voice. Alana couldn't make out what they were saying, but whatever it was, their laughter grew.

Rolling her eyes, Alana hobbled over and mouthed, "Move," elbowing her friend in the side.

With a dramatic gasp, Sofie backed off.

Her door, her apartment—she got dibs.

She lived in a luxury apartment building in downtown Cleveland, and the place was usually nice and quiet.

Until *he* brought home company.

Her neighbor was droolworthy, and she looked forward to the small glances she got of him occasionally.

Pushing her dark-rimmed glasses up the bridge of her nose, she stood on her toes to look through the peephole, which was placed high enough for people of average height, unlike her. Closing one eye, she focused on the figures standing in the hallway.

London Keith.

In the flesh.

Alana's breath caught in her throat as he came into view.

He was tall and muscular, with dark wavy hair.

He dripped sex appeal.

The nickname she and Sofie had chosen for him didn't do him justice.

Mr. Hotness.

And it appeared Mr. Hotness would be entertaining two bimbos tonight.

Alana took in their skimpy clothing and thin bodies. They were plastered all over London as he leaned back against the wall.

"What's going on?" Sofie whispered.

Alana's eyes grew wider as another woman came into view.

She swallowed hard.

He must have one hell of a dick.

"There's three of them tonight," Alana responded.

"Let me see." Pushing Alana aside, she peered through the hole.

Alana leaned back against the wall. Though he'd moved in a few months ago, they hadn't officially met. Every weekend, London brought home women who came and went. She noticed through all of her snooping that he never had the same one over. He was a man who loved women, and he didn't discriminate: tall, short, blonde, brunette, black, white, brown—he liked them all.

She'd never seen anyone who looked like her, though. Not that she was vying for London's attention or anything, but she'd be lying if she said she wasn't curious.

She was nothing like the women who were practically climbing him while he tried to get into his apartment.

Alana Thornton was shy, and proud to be called a nerd. Working as a financial analyst during the week, she loved hanging out, or reading at the trendy coffee shop a block away from her building on the weekends.

Coffee and books were where her heart was.

But lately, she yearned for more.

She wanted to become a woman men noticed.

A woman men desired.

"I can't ever see myself sharing a man," Sofie huffed.

The rumble of London's laughter echoed through the air before his door clicked shut, filling the room with silence.

London had moved his little party inside.

"They can have him," Sofie declared, pushing away from the door. Alana followed her back to the couch where their Scrabble game sat unfinished.

Saturday nights for them consisted of wine and board games.

The perfect dateless night with the bestie.

"Yeah, I don't think I could share, either. Half

the time, I don't even like sharing my ice cream with you," Alana retorted.

"Bitch." Sofie swung a pillow at Alana. Dodging it, she grinned, causing them both to fall into a fit of laughter.

"Hey, I'm just being honest."

Sighing, Sofie gripped the pillow to her chest. "I wouldn't want him as my man. Given the chance, would you spend one night with him? No strings attached? No one would ever have to know." Her perfectly arched eyebrow rose with her question.

Alana stared down at her glass, trailing a finger along the edge.

Would she?

One night to experience what London Keith had to offer?

She met Sofie's gaze. "Nope. His stick might be potent, but he ain't gonna have me strung out in these streets."

"I know that's right!" Easing off the couch, she headed toward the kitchen. "We need more wine."

Sofie had read her mind.

Leaning forward to rearrange her game pieces, Alana called out, "Hurry up so I can kick your butt!"

"Oh, no! I refuse to lose." Reappearing with the

bottle they had started, she refilled their glasses, set the empty bottle on the table, and took a seat. "For six bucks, this wine is good."

"Don't knock the cheap stuff. It tastes good, but will get you drunk fast," Alana joked. She was already feeling a warmth creep through her body, only she didn't know if it was from the wine or seeing London.

"So, where were we?"

"You were about to get your ass handed to you," Alana muttered, spelling out a new word.

Pushing the carnal thoughts of Mr. Hotness from her mind, she focused on the game before them.

There would be plenty of time to daydream about him.

Now, it was time to kick Sofie's ass.

Alana exited her bedroom, fresh from a shower. Sofie was long gone, having tucked tail and ran home.

Of course, Alana had won, again. As always.

Lately, Sofie had been encouraging Alana to work out with her. She'd gained about fifteen pounds in the last year and needed to shed it. Not that she wanted to get rid of all her curves, but she needed to get more active and healthier.

Working for Medical Health, an insurance conglomerate, she pulled a ton of hours each week, which didn't lend to healthy eating habits.

"What was I thinking?" she groaned.

Walking over to the coffee table, she cleared it of the empty bottle and glasses, but she couldn't shake off Sofie's question.

Would she give Mr. Hotness one night?

Not wanting to answer her own question, she placed the glasses in the sink and tossed the bottle into the recycling bin.

"I won't think of him," she sang aloud.

Who was she kidding?

Returning to the living room, she turned off the lamp and paused at the sound of laughter in the hallway.

"Good night, ladies."

She shuffled quietly to the door to find Mr. Hotness, shirtless, standing in his doorway.

Holy mother of God.

Her mouth watered at the sight of him. Even through the small hole, she could see the lines running down his abdomen and into his shorts, along with the muscles of his well-defined chest.

Watching him turn in her direction, she held her breath, as though he could hear her breathing while her heart started to race.

A voice in the back of her mind whispered... *what if?*

Stepping away from the door, she looked at herself in the mirror. She wore her satin bonnet, a cami, and a pair of boy shorts, with her oversized frames resting low on her nose.

Glancing back at the door, she sighed.

What she wouldn't give to not be a dependable employee, daughter, and friend.

She wanted to let her hair down. To be one of those giggling women ready for a night of sweating up the sheets with a hot guy.

She'd lied to Sofie.

She'd do it.

Only once.

There was no room in her life for fantasies of such a man.

Someone like London Keith wouldn't give her a second look. Women like her wouldn't be on his radar.

"Get your head out of the clouds, Alana."

Turning on her heels, she headed toward her bedroom.

She'd be better suited coming up with a good excuse to not go running with Sofie in the morning.

"Good night, and good riddance, Mr. Hotness," Alana whispered.

*L*ondon Keith stared at the door across from his. He couldn't shake the feeling that eyes were on him anytime he came and went.

His gaze swept the hallway and landed on the security camera posted in the far corner.

Maybe it was just his imagination.

Shrugging, he entered his apartment.

He'd moved in a few months ago, and he had to admit, it was the best idea he'd had in a long while. The luxury condo fit his exquisite tastes, allowing him to wine and dine potential clients right in the heart of the city.

Downtown Cleveland was a growing metropolitan area. Located on Lake Erie, it was home to popular restaurants, amazing night life, and was the central location of all the sports teams.

And that was the primary reason London had moved to his current home.

Sports.

He owned Primetime Sports Management, catering to professional athletes. His agency was one of the most successful ones out there, representing a majority of the top contenders in every sport.

With his success came riches and popularity—and women. Lots of women.

Last night was one for the books.

Models.

Three wild, kinky ones.

Walking into the kitchen, he smiled at the memory of his recent fuck session.

Even he had to admit they tested his stamina.

But now it was time to think of the upcoming week. It was courting time, and he had a slew of meetings lined up with potential clients he was looking forward to signing.

Setting his coffee cup down on the counter, he quickly put away the items he'd bought from the store. This was going to be a big year for his company, and there were a few files he needed to go over.

He and Jaxon, his business partner and brother, wanted to kick things up a notch.

Rumor had it, Khalil Roads, the number one draft pick in the professional basketball league five years ago, was said to be looking for a new agent, and his contract was about to end.

Snagging Khalil would be a dream.

Not only was he the top player, he was a goldmine.

With the endorsements London could help him get, he was more confident he could make not only Khalil richer, but himself as well.

Pouring coffee into his mug, he made his way into the living room and flopped down onto his couch. Placing his cup next to him on the end table, he reached for his laptop and got lost in his work.

Just as he was sending an email off to his secretary, he heard a muffled cry.

"What the…" He went quiet, trying to hear where the sound came from. Glancing down at his watch, he saw it was a little after eleven in the morning. He'd worked three hours straight.

Setting his laptop on the couch, he got up to investigate.

The cry sounded again, causing him to rush to the door. Yanking it open, he found a nice, shapely ass pointed in his direction.

"Nice ass," he muttered in appreciation.

She flew up to a standing position and fell into the wall.

"Pardon me?" she gasped, her large glasses magnifying her almond-shaped eyes. They were captivating, drawing him in. Her warm brown skin was damp with a fine sheen of sweat. Her long dark hair was gathered into a ponytail. His gaze made its way down her curvy frame dressed in a tank and the shortest of shorts that had given him something to fantasize about.

A whimper escaped her and it was then he noticed she was grasping her calf muscle.

"Can I help you with something?" he asked, stepping out into the hallway.

A pained expression crossed her face. "Uh, can you get the door?"

"Sure."

Helping her from the wall, he wrapped an arm around her waist, ignoring how well she fit against him with her soft curves.

"My keys are in my pocket," she murmured.

He bit back a curse. Sliding his fingers along the edge of her waistband, he connected with the tiny hidden compartment and pulled out her key.

"Got it," he whispered. His gaze met hers, and he could have sworn his heart skipped a beat. The urge to close the gap between them and get a taste of her—

"Charley horse," she exclaimed before crumpling over in pain, almost causing London to lose his hold on her.

"Gotcha." Pulling her in close, he slid the key into the lock and opened the door. Swooping her up into his arms, he pushed his way into her home. "Which way?"

He took in the home that was similar to his.

"The couch."

He strode forward and made his way into the living room, ignoring how right it felt to have her in his arms.

"Here we go, m'lady." He slowly lowered her down on the plush couch, feeling her gaze on him. Kneeling down before her, he slid his hands along her leg, finding the muscle tense. "London," he announced, kneading her calf.

"What?"

"My name. It's London. I figured I should introduce myself, seeing how I'm offering up a free massage."

She looked away, but not before he caught sight of her small smile.

"What's your name, pretty lady?" he asked, thickening his Southern drawl. As he continued to gaze upon her, he realized she was more than beautiful.

She was a knockout.

And he wanted to get to know her.

Intimately.

Her smooth skin was soft like butter beneath his fingers. When he caught her wince again, he eased up on the pressure.

"Alana Thornton." She turned back to him, her large eyes filled with curiosity. He had to look away, feeling the familiar stirring in his groin. His cock grew thick, pushing against his jeans.

"Nice to meet you, Alana Thornton," he replied, comparing her dark skin to his.

It was a complete turn-on.

Sliding his hands up along her leg, he stopped at her knee before gliding back over her now relaxed muscle.

He couldn't look away from the sight before

him. Her generous breasts pushed against her soft T-shirt, showcasing her erect nipples.

Her curvy body was perfect.

Soft.

Womanly.

Her eyes were closed as she relished in the feel of his hands on her.

What would she look like climaxing on my cock?

He swallowed hard, pushing away the image of her naked, braced over him, riding him. "How does it feel now?"

"Amazing," she moaned. Her muscles tensed again as a look of complete horror came over her face.

A hearty laugh exploded from his lips. He couldn't remember the last time he'd laughed so hard at someone else's expense.

"Good. I always aim to please." Releasing her, he stood up, running a shaky hand through his hair. "What you need is water, and a banana for potassium. Do you have any?"

"Yeah—"

Not waiting for her to finish, he headed toward the kitchen. He had to get away from her before he did something crazy, like pull her up from the couch and kiss her.

Grabbing a banana off the counter, he opened her fridge and pulled out a bottle of water.

He blew out a deep breath, trying to will his cock to calm the fuck down, which made him chuckle. It wouldn't do him any good to help his sexy neighbor with his cock drilling its way through his pants.

"You really don't have to do this," she said as he entered the living room.

Handing her the banana, he took a seat on the coffee table in front of her. "What kind of neighbor would I be?"

When she smiled, he noticed a small dimple in her right cheek.

There was no way he could watch her bite into the banana. It would only lead his thoughts down a slippery slope to see her place the tip of the fruit between her lips…

He looked around the room instead, taking in the decor. Her apartment was tastefully decorated in warm, inviting colors, giving off the homey vibe his was devoid of. The condo wasn't his primary home, but it allowed him to be close to work and all the things he loved about Cleveland.

He'd bought a home in the suburbs when he

first moved to Northeast Ohio, but it was massive, and he felt alone when it was just him.

It was meant for a family—a husband, a beautiful wife, and children.

"Lived in Cleveland long?" he asked, focusing back on her. Watching her set the empty peel down on the couch, he twisted the cap off the bottled water and handed it to her.

Nodding, she took a sip and told him, "I know you moved in a few months ago. Sorry I haven't been over to introduce myself."

"Don't worry about it." He stood and walked over to a picture hanging on the wall that caught his attention. It was a beautiful abstract painting with bold colors. "Wow. This is beautiful."

"Thanks. I got it from a starving artist auction a couple of years ago."

"Art buff?" Glancing over his shoulder, he found she had tucked her legs underneath her as she watched him.

"A little. Cleveland has a phenomenal art museum I like to go to."

"Maybe we can go together sometime." The words had spilled out before he even knew he was going to say them.

"Sure. We can do that one day."

He strode around, taking in all her photos of friends and family before making his way back over to her.

"All better?"

"Yes. Listen, I'd like to repay you for your help—"

"No need—"

"Do you like lasagna?"

He froze in place.

Could this gorgeous woman cook too?

"Who doesn't?"

"I make a mean lasagna, if I say so myself. I can bring you a plate to show you my appreciation before you go out tonight."

He was curious as to how she knew he'd be heading out later, but kept that question to himself.

"An offer that tempting would be hard to refuse."

She grinned at him, and he felt as if he'd been kicked in the chest. Her smile blew him away.

"Then once it's done, I'll bring you some."

With a quick nod, he walked to the door, Alana trailing behind him. Reaching past him, she opened it and stared up at him.

He held out his hand. "It's nice to meet you, Alana."

Placing her small one into his, she grinned. "You too."

"If you need another massage, don't hesitate to call," he joked.

"I'm sure I'll be fine." She bit her lip, and it took everything in him to keep from making his way back to her. Those lips of hers were calling to him. He wanted to taste them, to see if they were as sweet as they looked.

Walking backward through the hall and to his door, he kept his eyes on her as he turned the knob.

He'd offer her a free massage, all right.

A full body one.

With both of them naked.

"I mean it. I'm just a holler away."

With a wink, he turned and entered his apartment, closing the door behind him.

Alana didn't know whether she was more mortified of almost falling on the floor after her run with Sofie, or nearly having an orgasm on the couch in front of London.

That man's hands were God's gift to women.

She assumed he was a businessman, but those callouses told of a different side to him.

Just thinking of those large hands sliding along her skin sent a chill down her spine.

What would they feel like sliding along my naked breasts?

"Stop it!" she scolded herself.

But she couldn't forget how he'd picked her up with ease and carried her into her apartment, like she weighed nothing. She'd felt secure and feminine in his arms.

Fanning herself, she stepped out of her bedroom and walked through her home toward the kitchen.

Since she had bragged about her lasagna, she was going to have to take a trip to the grocery store to get all the necessary ingredients.

After London had left, Alana had made a beeline for the shower, where she almost had a heart attack once she got a look at her reflection.

Taking her time, she showered and washed her hair.

Now feeling like a new woman, she had a few things to accomplish before getting dinner done.

Snagging a pad and pen, she went through the cupboards and fridge, taking stock of what she had. She sighed in relief when she realized there wasn't much she would have to purchase.

With that done, she decided to get some work done. Her normal Saturday routine was to spend a few hours at her favorite coffee shop. She was working on a project in addition to her normal work requirements, and she usually spent a little of her time on the weekends to do it.

Later, she'd make her way to the store to get what she needed for their dinner date.

"It's not a date!" Storming out of the kitchen, she gathered up her laptop and other items she would need to take with her, muttering, "I'll ignore his muscles."

She'd gotten a quick feel of them when he'd carried her inside.

Muscle-clad men were her weakness, but not her norm. Her past boyfriends were just as nerdy as she was.

But it never stopped her from daydreaming about men like London.

London wouldn't be sexually interested in a woman like her. She was nothing like the women parading in and out of his apartment.

"This is just a kind gesture for not letting me fall flat on my face," she reminded herself.

Grabbing a jacket, she hoisted her bag up on her shoulder and left her apartment.

The weather was on her side. The sun was high in the sky, its rays warming the air around her.

Pushing her glasses up on her nose, she paused

at the corner of the street and waited for the light to change. Traffic wasn't as heavy on the weekends.

Alana loved living downtown. The high-rise buildings, local events, and the community attracted her to the area.

Nodding to a few pedestrians passing by, Alana made her way to her favorite coffee shop, 216 Beans. It was owned by a friendly woman named Peggy, who by far made the best coffee in town.

"Alana!" Peggy's warm, friendly voice called out as she entered the small establishment.

"Hey, Peggy Sue! How are you?"

With a smile, she walked up to the counter, ecstatic there wasn't anyone in line. This time of day, the coffee addicts thinned out a bit.

"Your usual?"

Reaching for her wallet, she laughed. "Of course." Alana was a regular, and she and the staff were on a first name basis.

Pushing her glasses up again, she turned and saw an open table near the front windows.

"Here you go, my dear," Peggy announced, grabbing Alana's attention.

Handing over a few bills, she eyed the cheese danishes. "These smell divine." Peggy's cheese danishes were famous. They were large and flaky, and the cream cheese was heavenly.

Peggy was a jolly older woman with white hair she pulled up into a bun on top of her head. Her tan weathered skin told she was a woman who didn't shy away from laughing.

"Why do you waste your time working on Saturdays? A young woman like you should be out there enjoying life."

Alana shrugged and took a sip of her coffee. Perfect. "I have some projects I'm working on. I figure I'll work hard now, and play harder later."

"Smart girl," Peggy affirmed. "Though what you need is a beau. Someone to spoil you rotten and put a certain type of gleam in your eye."

Alana snagged her danish off the counter, trying to keep herself from choking on her laughter.

"I'm trying, Ms. Peggy." With that, she turned and walked toward the empty table.

If only Ms. Peggy knew how Alana had been lusting after her sexy neighbor.

Sitting down, she set up her work station and dove into the files, but a certain cocky grin kept coming to mind and breaking her concentration.

Leaning back in her chair, she grabbed her coffee and sipped the delicious java while staring out the window, getting lost in her thoughts of London. As much as she needed to work, she just couldn't get him out of her head.

His sharp gray eyes. His dark locks, just long enough for a girl to run her fingers through.

Finishing her drink, she glanced at her watch. She'd wasted two hours and had barely touched the mountain of work she had wanted to plow through.

She might as well give up. Packing up her bag, she decided to head to the market.

She had a dinner to make.

"When's your meeting with Khalil?" Jaxon inquired.

Speaking with his younger brother on the phone, London leaned against the windowsill, gazing out at the beautiful blue sky.

The two Keith brothers were as close as could be. London was the oldest and loved torturing his younger brother.

They were raised in a small Southern town of Anniston, Alabama. Their parents, Phil and Nora Keith, were blue-collar workers who ensured

London and Jaxon had everything they could possibly need when they were children.

Where Jaxon had been a star baseball player, London had been an elite football quarterback.

Both had used their talents to gain full rides to college.

Upon graduating, London knew he didn't want to pursue playing football professionally. Though he'd been recruited, life in the league just wasn't for him. His brother, however, signed to play profession baseball.

London realized he wanted to manage players. It was a way for him to merge his love of sports with a profitable way to make money and save his body from the brutality of football.

Sports management.

It was something he was good at.

After obtaining a job at a small firm, he decided to branch out on his own.

His first client—his baby brother.

Jaxon had been doing well in the league, and London had landed a few endorsement deals that ensured his brother would never have to work again once his sports career was over.

That ending came way too soon.

One injury led to a string of others, and within a few years, Jaxon had to give up the bat.

But it wasn't the end of Jaxon in sports.

He too had got a business degree, and joined London at PSM.

London was only too happy to have his brother join the company. Together, they'd built Primetime Sports Management into what it was today.

"We're waiting for the season to end," London replied, running a hand along his face.

A light fragrance floated through the air.

Alana.

Her perfume still clung to his shirt.

He had spent the day trying not to think about his sexy, nerdish neighbor.

He wasn't sure when he started finding nerdy types sexy, but Alana had it in spades. With her, it wasn't a bad thing.

"And you're sure you have it all in the bag? Do you need me there?"

"I think I know what I'm doing," London scoffed, moving away from the window. Settling down on his couch, he put his feet up on the coffee table.

"I'm just saying, someone like Khalil may need

to have a former professional player help him sign with PSM."

London rolled his eyes at Jaxon's cockiness.

"While you were still in the leagues, I was signing players. I already have a relationship with Khalil. It'll be fine. I'm sure he's going to sign with us."

London and his organization had a reputation for getting hefty endorsement deals for their players, as well as for their integrity and business sense. PSM was not a company all about the money. They really cared for their players and made them all feel as if they were one big happy family.

"Got any plans tonight? I tried calling you last night, but you never answered. You must've been busy," Jaxon snorted.

"Yeah, I had my hands full." He didn't want to think about last night. It was nothing in comparison to the short time he'd spent with Alana.

"How many?"

Visions of Alana's smile flashed before him.

"It doesn't matter. When are you coming into town?"

"I should be there in about a month or so, give or take. I'm wrapping things up here first. If I had to choose between Los Angeles and Cleveland, I'd take Cleveland any day. Traffic is a beast out here."

London chuckled. It was hard getting used to the city life when you came from the country. Their town only had four traffic lights, and a handful of stop signs. Even though both of them had traveled the world over, they still preferred the slower pace of life.

That was another reason London settled his home office in Cleveland. He could get city life and country life in Northeast Ohio.

"Don't work too hard."

"What did you just say? I know you aren't telling me not to work hard," Jaxon exclaimed. "I'm sure you were working today, on the weekend."

"I was just reviewing—"

"I knew it! Put up the laptop, big brother. Search through your contact list and decide on a woman to call. Pick her up, wine and dine her, then fuck her. Have a great time."

London took in his brother's advice, and it was then he realized something.

He could care less about fucking some nameless woman.

The one he desired was located right across the hall.

And her number was not in his contact list.

Well, that would have to be rectified tonight.

"Nah. For once, I'm staying in," he mumbled. "I have something better in mind."

"Oh? What the hell is that?"

"None of your business. Fuck off."

Disconnecting the call, he tossed his cell onto the couch next to him.

His brother didn't need to know about Alana. He would ask too many questions.

London wasn't sure what this was between them, but he felt an attraction.

He was sure she did too.

There was no way the air between them could be that electric and she not feel it.

Getting to his feet, he strolled into his bedroom, wanting to test it again. See if what he felt earlier was still there.

Somehow, he knew it would be.

"Don't burn the bread. Don't burn the bread," Alana chanted. She was just finishing tidying up so it wouldn't appear to look like World War III had started in her kitchen.

The smells wafting through her apartment were divine. Throwing the last bowl into the dishwasher, she turned, satisfied with her accomplishment.

She was proud of her state-of-the-art kitchen. It was one of the perks of living in the building. Everything was top-notch, from the appliances to the marble countertops. The luxury condo was worth every penny.

One good sniff, and the hint of burning bread hit her.

"No!" Grabbing the mitt, she slid her hand inside and opened the door. A sigh of relief escaped her. "Perfect."

Sitting the pan on the counter to cool, she looked down at herself. If she was going to take a plate over to him, she'd better put on a nicer outfit.

Running into her bedroom in full panic mode, she flung open her closet door and stared at her clothes. Everything she had was for the office or lounging, as it was rare for her to go out. Her usual go-to were jeans and a cute top.

"Apparently, I need to go shopping."

She eyed her cell phone charging on the nightstand, tempted to call Sofie, but she couldn't tell her she was making dinner for London. Her best friend would want every detail on how she came to be cooking for Mr. Hotness.

"Jeans it is," she uttered, pairing them with an off the shoulder black top and flip flops.

It wasn't like she was leaving the building. She was just going to pack up a plate and take it across the hall to her neighbor as a thank you for helping her when she was in a load of pain.

Her heart sped up as she assessed herself in the

mirror. She'd put on a little mascara, lip gloss, and changed her glasses from black to her pearly white frames. They complimented her complexion quite nicely.

Alana had a small addiction to glasses. She'd wasn't one who could wear contacts, and the thought of laser eye surgery made her shudder.

So she was stuck with glasses, and she had a pair in every color.

She wasn't the type of woman who wore a ton of make-up like the ones coming and going from London's apartment. Alana liked to think she had natural beauty.

She had to admit, she was probably going over-board, but she wanted to look better than she had this morning in shorts and a tank top, all sweaty.

Now here she stood, her dark hair tumbling past her shoulders and looking good.

"Okay, Alana. We're going to make him a plate and carry it over to his apartment. That's it."

With her head held high, she walked out of her bedroom, feeling the signs of nervousness creeping up on her. She inhaled deeply and tried to will her heart to slow down.

When a knock sounded at the door, she froze.

"Who could that be?"

The building had a doorman who would buzz her first, should any guests show up.

Arriving at her door, she stood on her tiptoes and froze. Peering through the peephole, she couldn't believe who stood on the other side of her door.

London Keith.

Swinging open the door, she prayed she appeared nonchalant when she greeted him with, "Hey."

"Hope I'm not too early or too late. You never told me what time dinner was."

He leaned against the doorframe, his lopsided grin tugging at her heartstrings.

Dressed in a black button-down shirt and dark jeans, he oozed sex appeal.

Alana didn't think he could look bad in anything he wore. He could be dressed in a burlap sack and she'd want to tear it off of him.

His gaze wandered up and down her body, and her heart skipped a beat.

What was he thinking? She had to keep from fidgeting in place.

"I figured you'd be busy or something. I was going to bring... You know what? Never mind. Please, come in." If this man showed up to eat dinner, she wasn't going to send him away. She'd just have to improvise.

"I didn't want to come empty-handed. I hope you like red wine," he said, handing her the large bottle.

"I love red wine." She looked down at the seemingly expensive bottle—Gaja. She made a mental note to look up the name later. "I've never heard of this brand before."

"It's really good. One of my favorites," London informed her, following her into the kitchen. "I must say, I'm impressed by your kitchen. It looks like it gets a lot of use."

Setting the bottle on the counter, she looked up at him and grinned. "You don't cook?"

"When I have to, I can throw something together. Growing up, my mother tried to teach me, but it was like my brain processed nothing." He leaned against the counter. "But I can place an order for delivery like no one you've ever seen before."

She chuckled. "Well, I guess it's a good thing I offered to cook."

"I'll be forever in your debt." Unbuttoning his sleeves, he folded them up, presenting his forearms. "What do you want me to do?"

Alana swallowed at the sprinkling of light hair running along his tan skin that led to a tattoo peeking out from the fabric. There was something so sexy about a man's tattoos that did it for her.

Down, girl.

"If you want, you can set the table," she replied, finding her voice.

Looked like they were having dinner at her place.

She gave him instructions on where everything was while she gathered the food and carried it into the dining room.

Once she'd placed the salad and bread on the table, she went back for the lasagna.

Alana had to admit that finishing off dinner and working with London to get the table set just felt… right.

Something so simple had her core clenching.

She needed to get laid.

That was it.

The little things, like a man standing in her kitchen, shouldn't be turning her on.

"Where's your wine opener?" he asked, searching her utensil drawer. Her gaze landed on the wine bottle and she giggled. She normally bought the cheap stuff at the local grocery store that cost no more than six bucks, and it certainly didn't have a cork.

"I know I have one somewhere around here…" She turned around in a circle. "A-ha!"

Rushing to the fridge, she snatched it off the door and did a celebratory dance.

"Magnetic? Cool way not to lose it."

Nervous flutters filled her stomach as they walked back into the dining room. People had always told her what a great cook she was, so she was curious to see what London thought.

Piling up their plates and filling their glasses, she took a seat across from him.

"As soon I smelled this from my apartment, I couldn't wait to get over here."

"So what do you do?" she asked as they started in on their salads.

"I own Primetime Sports Management—a sports agency."

"Oh, wow. That sounds amazing. Do you work with professional athletes?"

She knew little about that world, but from what she saw on television and in movies, London's line of work was quite lucrative.

Being a sports agent had to mean London didn't want for anything financially. She'd heard that agents got a percentage of their athletes' monies, and if the client signed a crazy contract, London would reap in the benefits.

That was how he could afford the condo in their building.

And it certainly explained the beautiful women.

Alana, on the other hand, used money from her inheritance to buy her luxury home. Her parents, God rest their souls, had died a few years ago, a year apart from each other.

Her father, Max Thornton, had died from a long, drawn-out fight with colon cancer. Her mother, Anna Thornton, was said to have died from a broken heart almost a year to the day her beloved husband had died.

Between her parents' life insurance policies, Alana—as long as she budgeted—could live her life comfortably, while supplementing it with her income from her job.

"I'm the one who helps negotiate on behalf of my clients for their contracts and endorsements." Reaching for his wine, London took a hefty sip. "My work is boring. What about you? What does Alana do for a living?"

"Nothing as interesting as you," she snickered. "I work for Medical Health as a financial analyst. My job would really bore you. If you ever have trouble falling asleep, I can come over and start talking about what I do. I guarantee you'll be out like a light in no time."

London barked a laugh, and she felt a small smile playing on her lips. When he cut into the lasagna, she watched anxiously as he lifted it to his lips.

Closing his mouth around the fork, his eyes fluttered closed.

She needed to get laid.

Quick.

Fast.

And soon.

She shouldn't be close to orgasm watching a sexy man enjoy his food.

Food that she cooked for him.

"Alana," he groaned before opening his eyes.

She gave him a smile. "I'm glad you like it."

"Like it? Jesus, woman, I'm in love."

Relieved, Alana dug into her food, not batting an eye when London went in for seconds, and a third helping.

The wine bottle was soon empty, as were their plates.

Alana wasn't sure when they'd made it to the

couch. They'd turned the television on to a movie, but they ignored it, talking the night away.

She had learned much about him. Not only did he run the company, but his brother worked with him. He spoke of his college football days, which explained his perfect physique.

She felt comfortable and relaxed with London. They were sharing some of their most embarrassing stories from their teenage years.

"I don't believe it."

"I swear, I never thought my hair would grow back." She chuckled, thinking of the time she and Sofie had given each other perms. The chemicals were too strong and burned Alana's hair. She had been left with a large patch missing in the back, and she ended up having to cut her hair pixie short. "The painful things women have to go through to look beautiful."

"Glad I'm not a woman." London shook his head, smiling. "I don't think I can go through what you all do."

Alana wasn't sure when they had gotten so close to each other. London's arm was lying across the back of the couch, and she was practically tucked into his side.

He studied her, just as she took the time to do the same to him.

Reaching up, she tucked a wayward strand of hair behind his ear and whispered, "This was fun."

"It was," he agreed, his gaze dropping to her lips, which suddenly felt as dry as the desert. Running her tongue along them, his stormy gray eyes grew dark.

This was new territory for her.

Sure, she'd had boyfriends in the past, but none of them could hold a candle to London.

Her last boyfriend, Danny, wasn't a physical type of guy. The only muscles he worked were the ones in his hands and arms when he played video games. He was a gamer who spent countless hours in front of his television.

When she tried to get him to workout with her, his asthma always got in the way.

Swallowing hard, she tore her gaze away and looked down at her watch. It was a little after midnight.

"It's getting late," she exclaimed, getting to her feet.

Where did the time go?

"Really?" Standing, he ran a hand through his hair. "It's only a little after twelve."

"Only? I must be getting old," she muttered, walking into the kitchen with their empty glasses. She wasn't sure when thirty-two became old, but midnight was past her bedtime.

"If you want, I can run over to my place and grab another bottle—"

"London, it's late."

"You're right, I should go. You sure you don't want me to help clean up?"

"I'm positive. Besides, there isn't much to do."

Ushering him out of the kitchen, she led him toward the door. Entering the hallway, London turned to her and slid his hands into his pockets as they stared at each other in a comfortable silence.

His gaze dropped to her lips before meeting her eyes once more.

"Thanks for dinner. Next time, it's on me."

She gave him a genuine smile. "Okay."

"Lock your door so I can make sure you're safe, Alana."

"Good night," she whispered as she gripped the handle, afraid she'd do something she would regret later.

Like kiss him.

"Good night, Alana."

Closing the door, she rested her forehead against it.

Having him over was a big mistake.

Now that his manly energy was in her home, she'd never be able to stop thinking of him.

At the moment, she didn't want to.

"I must be out of my mind."

Running a hand over his face, he set his empty cup down on the counter.

His dreams had been plagued with images of Alana.

Last night, he didn't want to leave her presence. He couldn't remember the last time he'd enjoyed just hanging out with someone.

A female, no less.

One he didn't sleep with.

He was attracted to her. There was no doubt about that.

Her sweet personality, shyness, her smile, and those damn glasses captivated him.

She wasn't like the other women he usually surrounded himself with.

She was different.

A breath of fresh air.

Moving to the door, he peered through the peephole.

No signs of anyone in the hallway.

"I'm officially a stalker now," he muttered, pushing away from the door.

Even if she were to appear, what would he do? Run out there? And then what?

Making his way into the living room, he turned on the TV. The NBA Finals were on, and Khalil's team had made it in last night with their win. If he won the championship, his value would increase tenfold.

With London representing him, he'd ensure the basketball star got paid every penny he was worth, and then some.

Pulling up the game he'd recorded last night, he started to watch. It would help for him to be up on all the games so far, and important for him to become familiar with Khalil's style of play.

After a few moments into the game, he caught

the sound of a door opening in the hallway. Vaulting over the couch, he snatched up his keys and wallet off the table and opened his door.

Alana gasped and turned around, hefting her bag up on her shoulder.

"Hey, London."

"Hey, Alana." Smiling, he put on a calm and collected appearance as he shut and locked his door before fully turning to Alana. After a few moments of studying each other in silence, they broke out into a fit of laughter. "What, might I ask, do you have planned for today?"

He took notice of her pink and purple glasses. Her hair was long, flowing around her shoulders. She was dressed in a long T-shirt that stopped just below her ass over a pair of leggings.

"I'm off to do some work. I can't concentrate here because I get distracted by things that need to be done. I'll see dishes in the sink and have a desperate need to wash them, which will then lead to vacuuming and laundry. Before I know it, the whole damn day is gone." Her hands moved around theatrically as she rattled on, her lips turned up in a grin. He found himself grinning along with her. "So I leave and go to my favorite coffee shop. I also wanted to do a little knickknack shopping today."

"Mind if I join you? I could use a good cup of coffee and stretch my legs." She tugged her bottom lip between her teeth, causing the arousal he felt for her to blossom. "You can show me some of the cool spots in the area."

Her grin grew. "I don't mind at all."

London settled into walking alongside her toward the elevator, slowing his stride to match hers.

The ride down was quiet. Exiting into the lobby, they made their way outside. It was the weekend, and traffic was light. Having a break from the normal hustle and bustle of downtown life through the week was quite nice.

Alana pointed out little quirky shops, with a story to tell for each one. She captivated him, and he found himself drawn into her world. He'd walked the neighborhood quite a few times, but hadn't really seen it until now.

"Here's the best coffee shop around. And Peggy's danishes are to die for," Alana gushed.

London took in the scents flowing around them, and his stomach rumbled.

"You had me at best coffee shop." Placing his

hand at the curve of her back, he grabbed the door handle and moved aside for her to enter.

"Thank you," she murmured, walking past him. Following her in, he kept his hand in place.

The small touch fed his craving for her.

A satisfying feeling spread throughout his chest when she didn't move away from him. Her floral scent was now masked by the sweet smells of the baked goods.

But he'd memorized the perfume.

He wanted to know what it was so he could potentially buy stock in it.

"Alana!" a voice called out.

"Hey, Peggy!" Alana waved excitedly as they walked up to the counter.

"And who is this with you?" the older woman inquired, arching her brow at Alana.

A shyness came over Alana. It must have been his ancient caveman ancestors that made him want to pound on his chest with the knowledge that she didn't bring other men to the shop.

Laughing nervously, she tucked a strand of hair behind her ear. "Peggy, this is my neighbor, London. London, this is Peggy, the woman who owns this marvelous shop. One taste of her danishes and you'll be hooked."

"How are you?"

He held back a chuckle as the woman blushed.

"I'm doing well. What can I get ya'll?"

"How about you order for me?" he asked, turning to Alana. Her eyes grew wide behind her glasses.

"Really?"

"Surprise me."

She ordered two coffees. To him, it sounded like she was speaking in a foreign language. His usual order was just black, but he wanted to see what type of drink and food she would pick out for them.

"Your total is twenty-one dollars even," Peggy announced.

"I got this—"

"Not gonna happen," he said, pulling out his wallet after gently pushing her away from the counter.

"Hey," she scoffed, trying to push him to the side, but he stood firm.

"Nope. My treat."

He handed Peggy his credit card as she laughed at Alana's antics of trying to get around him.

Wrapping his arm around her waist, he pulled her to his side.

"You don't have to pay for me," she breathed, staring up at him.

It didn't get past him that she hadn't moved from his side. He slid his arm up her back and rested it along her shoulders.

"I want to. Plus, you cooked dinner last night." He turned to find Peggy with a shit-eating grin on her face. "I can pick up the tab for breakfast this morning."

"Sign here, son." She turned her attention to Alana. "You cooked him dinner, huh?"

"I was repaying him for his help," Alana advised through a long, exaggerated sigh.

"She cooked lasagna," he bragged. Peggy's eyebrows shot up even farther. "It was the best fucking lasagna I've had in years."

"I was already making it, and I offered him some for helping me out," Alana explained.

"Let's see here if I can sign with my left hand," he muttered, not planning to release Alana to do it.

Giggling, she rested her hand on his chest. "Boy, you can let me go now."

"No way. I like you just where you are." He took the pen and scribbled where his name was to go. "See? I signed for it."

"Give me about another minute or so to get your food ready."

Laughing, Peggy turned away.

London looked around the establishment and found a few people on their phones or laptops, ignoring everything going on around them.

"Why don't I snag a table and you grab our order?" she suggested, her smile slowly disappearing from her face. His gaze dropped down to her plump lips. He'd give his left nut to taste them right now.

"That's fine."

Releasing her, he immediately missed the feeling of her pressed up against him. If he held on to her any longer, he couldn't promise he'd behave.

Alana sat down at her favorite booth in Peggy's store, where it allowed her to have a view of the city, and she could people watch. She placed her bag on the bench beside her.

Glancing up, she met London's steady gaze and waved.

She had been shocked and nervous when he'd asked if he could tag along with her. She hadn't known what to think.

Him grabbing her and keeping her flush at his side sent her body into a frenzy.

What was that all about?

Her body had just about gone up in flames. Her cheeks hurt from smiling so much. One look at Peggy's grin, Alana knew she'd have to explain who Mr. Hotness really was.

"Here we go," London drawled, setting their food and cups on the table. Her breath caught in her throat at the sound of his Southern drawl. She tried to curb her facial expressions, not wanting to look like a lovestruck fool.

"Thanks."

She watched him take the seat across from her. His eye color was unusual, captivating her. She couldn't look away from them.

"What kind of drinks did you order us?"

Alana blinked. Her cheeks warmed at being caught staring at him. Tucking her hair behind her ear, she motioned to their cups.

"Take a sip and tell me what you think."

Alana waited with bated breath as he sipped the coffee. She'd ordered him the same thing she always got—an Americano, heavy cream, sugar free vanilla, with a few packets of stevia.

She got an espresso—sweetness, with no hint of

carbs.

Alana had a sweet tooth, and in her mind, she balanced her meal with this drink and a danish.

Best of both worlds.

"Wow." He gave her an approving nod. "That is good. Not too sweet, but smooth."

"Glad you enjoy it. I order it every time I come here."

Taking a sip of her espresso, she sighed when the flavor coated her tongue.

"You come here often?" London asked. Leaning back, he watched her tear off a piece of the danish and put it into her mouth. His eyes darkened, his gaze settling on her lips.

She ran her tongue along her lips to clean off the stickiness of the glaze.

London picked up his identical danish and took a healthy bite. His eyes widened, and he took another bite before setting it down on the tray.

"This is dangerous."

Alana laughed. She had the same thoughts when she first stumbled upon the 216 Beans cafe.

"Exactly. This is why I need to work out. I've gained fifteen pounds since I moved downtown. All these danishes have gone straight to my hips."

"Hmm…" London murmured, causing her to

shift uncomfortably in her chair. She wasn't sure what he saw when he looked at her. Unconsciously, she pushed her glasses higher on her nose.

Last night…

She was sure he was going to kiss her, but she had chickened out by proclaiming it was late. Alana wasn't sure if she was brave enough to cross that line yet. She wasn't like those other women who came and went from his place.

"What's that supposed to mean?" she asked, though not sure why. Did she want to hear that she needed to lose weight? No. Not from him.

"I was going to say that I don't see any problems with you at all. I like you just the way you are." He met her gaze. There was no hint of a smile, or any inclination that he was joking.

Oh, shit.

He was serious.

"You're just saying that because you'll want more of my lasagna." A nervous chuckle escaped her. Popping the rest of the danish into her mouth, she chewed, trying to prevent herself from saying something else she'd regret.

"I'll always accept a good home-cooked meal from a beautiful woman."

His lips curled up into a smile, revealing his

perfect teeth. Looking relaxed, he reached for his coffee and took another sip.

Her heart raced.

He thought she was beautiful?

No fucking way.

A silly grin spread across her face.

"Keep talking like that, I'll have to make my chicken carbonara," she said with a wink.

Holy mother of God.

Did she just do that? She wasn't the flirty type, and didn't know who this person was taking over her body.

He looked at her over his cup and raised his brow. "Don't make me beg, woman."

He wouldn't ever have to beg for anything from her.

"Okay. I'll let you know the next time I make it."

Before long, they had finished their coffees. Alana wasn't sure how time had gotten away from her. She was supposed to be working, but she didn't want to. She wanted to be a little selfish. Here she had a man paying attention to her, offering pleasant conversation with a sexy Southern accent.

Butterflies filled her stomach.

What was this?

"So, where to next?"

She tilted her head and studied him. Well, she had planned to go knickknack shopping after work, but it looked like her plans were changing.

"There are a few shops I do want to stop in."

Clearing their table, London tossed their trash away before walking back over to her. Her core clenched at the swagger in his walk.

"Lead the way."

London couldn't take his eyes off Alana. She looked completely at home in the book/record shop. It had an indie, homey feel. Just stepping into the establishment had him feeling as though he'd stepped back in time.

"You still have a record player?"

He couldn't help but touch her. Her thick, dark hair was straightened, resting on her shoulders. When she looked up at him, her eyes were magnified by her pink and purple glasses.

Last night, they were a crisp white pair. Today's were colorful, hinting at her quirky personality.

"I do," she admitted. "There's something about the sound of a record that you don't get on digital."

"What are you looking for?" he asked, moving in closer to take in her floral scent. Her perfume was driving him crazy. He wanted to bury his face in the crook of her neck and breathe it in.

"Just browsing."

Picking up one, he chuckled. "Now this is a blast from the past."

Peeking at his choice, she burst into a fit of laughter. "What do you know about that?"

"My mother loved all kinds of music. She always had her records playing while she cleaned the house."

He ran his hand along the cover of the album, remembering his mother pulling her records out so she could put them on the turntable.

"Your mother played Bobby Caldwell?"

Feigning hurt, he placed his hand over his heart. "What's wrong with that?"

"I don't know. With that accent of yours…"

"Growing up in the country, sometimes all you did was listen to music. Even my father loved it. He'd bring out his guitar and play while we sat by the fire.

Memories of his youth surfaced, and it left him

feeling a little homesick. His parents were his and Jaxon's biggest supporters.

"Sounds like you had an amazing upbringing," she breathed.

"I did. My record collection is at home in my old room, collecting dust," he replied wistfully.

He made a promise to come back and take his time browsing, the smell of the records bringing back so many memories. He'd forgotten how much he loved just sitting around, listening to music.

He put back the album and followed her as she moved farther down the aisle.

"And what's my accent got to do with anything?" he questioned, needing to hear her explanation as to what his accent had to do with music.

She spun around and walked backward, away from him, her face lit up with merriment. In the two days he'd now spent with her, he was learning her mannerisms, and now she was in a playful mood he was enjoying immensely.

London felt the most relaxed he'd ever been. Most of his encounters with women were that of the physical kind, having no desire to get to know them.

Alana was different.

He wanted to know everything about her. Her inner thoughts when he caught her staring at him. The nerdy side of her. He even wanted to know more about the books she loved to read and the movies she liked to watch.

He had a great time last night, and hadn't wanted it to end.

But something happened. She had shut him down and sent him packing.

It had felt so good to have her tucked into his side. One second more on the couch, they would have kissed.

He didn't know what he had done wrong. She'd rushed him out of her apartment, leaving him confused. He had wondered if he had done or said something he shouldn't have, but after spending time with her today, he doubted it.

He had this deep ache in his chest to know what those plump lips of hers tasted like. What had thrown him off was that she thought she could do with losing some weight.

The idea was crazy.

Her plush body was like that of a Greek goddess, curvy in all the right places. He couldn't keep his hands off of her.

Desire for her warmed his body and flowed

down to his cock. It grew stiff and heavy watching her walk away from him.

"I just figured all you Southern boys were into country music."

A hearty laugh escaped him. That was a new one for him to hear. Yes, he was raised in rural Alabama, but that didn't mean they were hillbillies who only listened to country.

"Really? So you had me pegged for a good ol' Southern hillbilly?" He stalked toward her, enjoying their interaction. He knew he still spoke with an accent that gave away his Southern roots.

"By looks? No. When you thicken your accent up on purpose, like you're doing now, then yes," she replied haughtily.

She spun around on her heel and walked over to the book section, where rows of shelves lined the walls. The scent of paperbacks filled the air, reminiscent of the times he'd spent in the libraries in college studying for exams.

His gaze dropped to the swell of Alana's ass. His pants were now tight, and it was a struggle to keep from unzipping his jeans to give him some form of relief.

Maybe he was an uncultured hillbilly. No

woman had ever had this effect on him. He could normally control his urges, but being in Alana's presence changed all that.

He wanted her.

That was without question.

London didn't say a word as she watched him, her gaze darting to him as she browsed the books. Pulling one out, she flipped through the pages, moving her glasses up her nose before reading the blurb on the back. An unconscious move while she got lost in what she was reading.

The music playing floated along the airwaves, giving the shop a mellow, calming effect.

They were the only two in the area.

London stood behind her much shorter frame, causing her to stiffen before slowly turning around with curiosity in her eyes. He liked how much of a size difference there was between them. Most of the women he affiliated with were tall models, and that had been something he thought he was in to. But he was quickly finding out he liked short, curvy, nerdy women.

Before he knew what he was doing, he gathered her to him and lowered his head.

"London…"

Her breathless whisper was the only thing he heard. It did wicked things to his body that he couldn't explain.

Their lips met in a scorching kiss. It was hard, unforgiving, and deep. London was trying to hold on to his control, but it was slowly slipping away.

Her lips parted, allowing him to taste the sweetness that waited for him. The slight hint of her coffee lingered. His tongue slid along hers, stroking it gently. She met him shyly at first, but soon returned the kiss with the same fever he bestowed upon her.

Running his hand through her hair, he gripped the thick strands while tilting his head to deepen the kiss.

He needed more.

He swallowed Alana's moan as he drank her in, ignoring the sound of the book she was holding hitting the floor. Her hands slid up to hold on to his shoulders, her nails digging into his skin.

He tried to ease up on the feral kiss, but he was losing the battle.

Now that he'd gotten a taste of her, he wanted it all.

His other hand explored her soft body before making its way to the curve of her ass. He groaned, loving how she fit in his palm. She pushed up against him, his cock pressing against her stomach…

The sound of a cough behind them was like a splash of cold water on his face. He tore his mouth away and put himself in front of her. Looking over his shoulder, he found an older man giving them a disapproving glare.

"Are you buying something or not?" he growled.

"Sorry. Yes, we'll be purchasing a few books," London responded, feeling Alana rest her head against his chest. Clearing his throat, he added, "Newlyweds. Can't seem to keep my hands off of her."

The gentleman's face softened. "I understand, young fella. Make your purchases and take her home."

"Yes, sir."

He turned back to Alana once they were alone again. Her eyes were wide, with a hint of embarrassment.

"What's wrong?"

"We were just caught making out like teenagers in a library."

"Well, I'm not regretting any of it. I've been wanting to kiss you since I met you," he murmured, running his finger along her bottom lip.

Her eyes widened. "Really?"

Why did she seem shocked that he was attracted to her? She was a beautiful woman, and extremely sexy.

Didn't she see it?

"I'm sure you can feel how much I want you."

Not the least bit ashamed of his painful erection, he pressed it against her, ensuring she felt what she did to him.

Her brown eyes, magnified by her glasses, appeared to grow even wider.

"I did that to you?" Her lips twitched, trying to play innocent, but London read right through it. There was a little sex hellion inside of her. She appeared to be a cute nerd on the outside, but he could see what was waiting in the depths of her gaze.

"Alana, Alana." He blew out a deep breath and pushed her up against the bookcase, his hands resting on the shelves behind her while kissing her hard. "Know what would help me with this problem?"

She shuddered, desire and lust burning bright in

her eyes. She licked her lips, her focus remaining on him.

"What?"

"A good hard fucking. You and me." He pressed another kiss to her lips. "I want to be buried so far inside of you, we won't know where you start and I end."

$\mathcal{A}$lana wasn't sure when this turned into a date.

Well, they didn't officially call it a date, but if it walked like a duck and quacked like a duck…

She looked down at their entwined hands as they walked along the sidewalk.

They'd had their first argument at the register when it came time to pay for the books she'd wanted to purchase. London had insisted on paying for them, and she'd refused. But somehow, he got his way.

Memories of the kiss still lingered. Her heart

raced thinking of how he had basically kissed the life from her.

She had forgotten for just a moment that they were in a public place and had been ready to do whatever he wanted. Sexually frustrated and mortified, she'd hid her face in his shirt as he spoke with Ron, the salesclerk.

It had been a while since she'd felt the hardness of a man. Her previous partners didn't hold a candle to the one kiss she had shared with London.

God help her, she wanted him.

She wanted what he wanted.

I want to be buried so far inside of you, we won't know where you start and I end.

Her core clenched with the gruffness of his voice and the dirty promise of what could be.

"Where are we going now?" Alana asked. He had been following her lead, but now it would seem he was choosing where they would go next.

He slowed his pace, as her strides weren't as long as his.

Living downtown had its perks. There were plenty of shops and restaurants within walking distance. The skyscrapers, and the culture of downtown living was addicting.

"Well, since we went to two places you wanted

to go, I actually need to stop and pick up a few things." He motioned toward the shopping center, Tower City, a mixed facility composed of office buildings, shopping, and a casino.

Alana enjoyed browsing through the fancy stores. Once in a while, she would indulge herself and buy something expensive, but she preferred supporting the local Mom and Pop establishments.

"What type of things do you need?" she asked as they arrived at the entrance, where he opened the door for her. She brushed past him and entered the department store with him close behind.

"Well, I figured since I have a big meeting soon, I should get a new shirt and tie." He guided them through the high-priced store to the men's section. Her gaze landed on a few price tags, and she swallowed hard.

"I'm sure you'll want to look your best."

London reached back and took her hand in his. Bringing her to his side, he wrapped his arm around her shoulders.

Alana took notice of a few women dressed in heels and expensive dresses, all throwing appreciative glances toward London. But he paid them no mind.

"If I can land this deal, it'll be monumental for my company."

"Can I help you, sir?" a young woman inquired as she approached. She was tall and thin, with long blonde hair. Her make-up was flawless, and her dress showed off her slender figure. Everything about her screamed fake. She was all smiles, with her gaze locked on London. Not once did she glance Alana's way. "My name is Rebecca, and I'd be happy to help you."

Bitch.

Alana stiffened. Memories of the other women she had watched come and go from London's apartment came to mind.

Rebecca would fit right in with them.

This was the kind of woman he preferred.

Trying to step away from London, he tightened his hold on her.

"Yes, Rebecca. I'm looking for a nice dress shirt and tie for a meeting," London shared with the store associate. He offered a small smile, but it didn't quite reach his eyes.

"Why yes, I can help you with that." Her smile grew even brighter as she motioned for them to walk with her. "You can call me Becky. I didn't catch your name."

Wow. Becky was laying it on pretty thick with her megawatt smile, and she hadn't once looked at Alana.

"Because I didn't give it," he replied dryly. "It's London, and this is my dear friend, Alana."

"Nice to meet you both."

Alana blew out a deep breath and offered a fake smile of her own. If he needed to shop for a few things, she could go browse around so he wouldn't be distracted by her. It sounded as if this meeting was pretty important.

She tried to pull away, but this time, he entwined their fingers together. He frowned when she tried to pull away again.

"I can go look at some things while you're doing—"

"Nonsense. I want your opinion."

Tightening his hold on her hand, he tugged her to him, dropping a kiss on her forehead. "Stay with me. Please."

Alana met his gaze and felt herself falter.

That damn accent of his.

He knew what he was doing by laying it on thick.

Alana gave a jerk of her head. She would stay with him if it was what he wanted. She glanced at

Becky, who still had her fake smile in place, but Alana saw the hint of disappointment at not being alone with London in her eyes.

"Lead the way," she said, holding back a smirk.

Score one for Alana.

Becky was an attentive sales associate, presenting him with different colors and styles.

Finally, he settled on a black button-down.

Alana's mouth watered. She couldn't wait to see him in it.

"I think that was an excellent choice," Becky assured, motioning for them to follow her. "Let's go back over to the ties. I have the perfect color for you."

Following behind her, they stopped at one of the tables. Leaving them to it, Alana moved over to where the ties were presented on a velvet case, each lined up single file. She found one that reminded her of London's eyes. It was dark gray, and she instantly fell in love with it. The color would pair well with his shirt.

She fingered the material, finding it one of the softest she had ever touched. Turning over the tag, she paused. The tie was worth more than all of her utilities combined for one month.

Her arm jerked back, as if she'd been shocked.

"Find anything?" London's deep voice rumbled.

"Maybe. You?" she asked, seeing Becky at his side. A few other women lingered near the register, not hiding the fact that they were ogling London. Alana's gut churned at how bold they were, just staring and giggling like schoolgirls.

Her gaze moved back to London and found him waiting for her response.

"I think he should pick this one. It would contrast nicely with the shirt." Becky held up a navy-blue tie. It was nice, but it wasn't the one that would highlight his unique eyes.

"What do you think, Alana?"

"This might be a little expensive, but I really like this one."

She held up her choice, trying not to cringe at the thought of how much the small piece of material was. Moving close, he laid it across the shirt.

"I think this is the one."

"It matches your eyes," Alana said softly. London's eyes crinkled in the corners with his smile.

Turning, he handed the items to Becky. "We'll take these."

"Yes, of course." Becky scooped up the shirt and tie. "Would you like to look at suits? We have a fantastic sale going on today—"

"Just the shirt and tie," London interjected.

Before long, Becky had him rung up and ready to go. Alana was in shock at the amount he'd paid for the two items.

"What did you want to look at?" he asked her.

She blinked.

Oh, yeah. She was going to browse while he dealt with Becky.

"Well, I wanted to go to the perfume counter." Her favorite perfume was getting low, and she needed more.

Becky escorted them to the perfume and cologne counter, where one of the women who had been gawking at London was waiting. This one, Jennifer, was a little nicer than Becky, and very attentive to her.

When she'd asked if they had her favorite perfume, Jennifer immediately produced it for her.

"Can I smell it?" London asked.

"Of course."

Smiling, Jennifer sprayed a small amount on a white card and waved it in the air before handing it to London. Bringing it to his nose, he inhaled and closed his eyes.

"Is this what you wear?" he asked.

"It is. I discovered it in college and fell in love

with it. I'm so glad we found it here. I'm a little low, and would hate it if I ran out."

London turned to Jennifer. "We'll take it."

"Yes, sir."

Reaching into her shoulder bag, she took out her wallet.

"That'll be ninety-eight dollars even," Jennifer announced, placing the perfume into a fancy little bag with a cloth handle.

Alana went to hand over her credit card, but London beat her to it.

"I got this."

"No way," Alana exclaimed. He had already spent a small fortune on his shirt and tie, their breakfast, and her books.

"I insist. Please, Jennifer, put her purchase on my card."

"London—"

"It's final." Pulling her close, he wrapped his arm around her waist while Jennifer turned to the register and finished the transition. "It's not much, and I want to buy it."

"London—"

He placed a finger over her lips to silence her.

"Let me do this for you," he murmured.

Everything else ceased to exist in that moment.

All Alana could think about was London. He wasn't playing fair. The deepening of his voice, the feel of his hard muscles against her… it was scrambling her brain, and he knew it.

"Think of it as a neighborly gesture."

Neighborly gesture, my ass.

An hour ago, he had practically devoured her with only a kiss.

There was nothing friendly about what was happening between them.

She was in a world of trouble.

Just like that, he had her eating out of the palm of his hand.

"This was nice," Alana said, leaning against the door to her apartment.

She couldn't remember the last time she had spent a day with a member of the opposite sex. Danny didn't believe in shopping. Any new clothes he needed were ordered online from the same store. Presents for her consisted of tickets to Comic-Cons. Sure, he would purchase the flights and hotels, but that wasn't really what she considered a gift.

Once in a while, she wanted little trinkets or thoughtful presents. Just because she was nerdy, didn't mean she wasn't a woman.

Looking at London, she bit her lip.

In two days, she'd gathered that he was a Southern gentleman when he wanted to be, doing well financially, owned his own business, and was close with his family. It also didn't hurt that he was drop dead gorgeous, had a body like a god, and his kisses… She grew hot just thinking of the one they had shared.

She wanted more like that.

"This was fun. It's crazy to think I've been living here for months and never just walked around the neighborhood."

"What do you do when you're not working?"

"I go out, but never took advantage of what's nearby."

"Well, there are some great restaurants too. I've tried almost all of them at least once," Alana boasted. She had made it her mission to try each restaurant within walking distance. There were so many ethnic places to eat that one could think they were in a different country each night of the week.

"We'll have to try a few of them," he murmured, stepping closer.

"That would be fun."

When his cell phone rang, he pulled it out of his pocket and sent it to voicemail. It had been ringing all throughout the day, but he'd ignored it, giving all his attention to her.

He'd made her the center of his attention for the entire day, and that was rare.

She was always competing with video games when she and Danny were together. That had been the last straw for her with that relationship.

But London was different.

It was nice to have someone who listened to her, laughed at her corny jokes, and wanted to get to know her. She didn't want this day to end.

"You sure you don't want to get that?"

"Nah, I'm good. It felt nice to ignore work and the world for a day." He slid his phone back into his pocket and shook his head. "Jaxon has been getting on my case about not taking a day off."

"Jaxon's your brother, right?" she asked, tilting her head back against the door. He had moved closer to her, leaving only inches between them.

"Yup. Younger, and he thinks he can boss me around."

"I hear siblings are always a pain in the butt."

Not that she knew from personal experience. She was an only child, but had plenty of cousins and friends growing up. Sofie was one of four kids, and her stories of her siblings always kept Alana entertained.

"Can't kill them, can't live without them." Resting his hand on her shoulder, he trailed it down to her hand. "It would seem tonight, it would be my turn to provide dinner."

"But you bought our breakfast."

It was obvious he didn't want the day to end, either. Warmth flooded her at the thought of him enjoying her company as much as she did his.

"That can't compare to the dinner you cooked." His smile disappeared. "Why don't you come over. You can pick the movie, and I'll order pizza."

Dinner and a movie? It was official. Today had been a date.

"That sounds good. I just need to drop these inside and freshen up a bit."

She wasn't going to take a chance that dinner and a movie might go a little further.

She had to be prepared.

His eyes darkened as he kissed her lips. "Don't take too long."

"I won't. Ten minutes?"

He stepped back and grinned. "I'll start the clock."

Unlocking her door, she walked inside and

closed it behind her. Suddenly feeling weak in the knees, she rested her back against it.

Her heart pounded in excitement. Pushing off the door, she rushed toward her bedroom and tossed her things onto the bed. Kicking off her shoes, she flew over to her closet.

"Does Netflix and chill really mean sex?" she muttered aloud.

This was going into territory she wasn't familiar with.

Looking at her phone, she wondered if she should call Sofie.

No. Hell no.

If she did that, she'd have to explain yesterday and today. Her friend would never allow her to get off the phone. When they finally had this discussion, lots of wine would be needed.

Stripping out of her clothes, she went into her bathroom. She wasn't proud of herself, but she took a hoe bath.

"A girl always has to be prepared."

Walking back into her bedroom a few minutes later wrapped in a towel, she opened her dresser drawer and pulled out a set of sexy panties and bra she had purchased for a special occasion.

This purchase was made months ago in the hopes that one day, she'd have a dick appointment.

It looked like it might be the day.

Sliding the cool silk on her body, she tried to will her nerves to stay calm. If kissing between them was that electric, what was it going to be like once they took their relationship further?

She didn't want to seem too excited about their dinner and movie, so she put on leggings and a cute shirt before walking her to her dresser where she kept her glasses lined up. Tonight, she was feeling feisty, and picked out a red pair.

They matched her red shirt nicely.

Grinning, she slid on a pair of sandals and looked at herself in the full-length mirror.

"Subtle sexiness."

She looked perfect.

After running a brush through her hair, she was ready. Turning to leave, she paused at her bed. Grabbing the bag with the perfume London had purchased for her, she sprayed herself a few times.

He apparently liked the scent.

Grabbing her keys and cell phone, she got to the door and heard voices out in the hallway.

She peered through the peephole. A woman— tall, with long brown hair, who looked as if she had just stepped off a runway—entered London's apartment and closed the door.

Alana shut her eyes for a moment, hating the feeling spreading through her body. Leaning her head against the door, she tried to take a deep breath.

She couldn't believe she had blocked that piece of information out about him.

He was a player.

There was no way in hell she could compete with those women. She'd never be as tall, slender, or as beautiful as them.

She pushed off the door, angry at herself for letting him get to her, and mad for comparing herself to those floozies.

She could never compete with miniskirts and long legs.

She thought they had a connection.

Maybe she was just another woman to him. Men like London took what they wanted, and this weekend, he apparently wanted a little chubby, nerdy girl.

"Why are you here, Bianca?" London asked, pissed at her unexpected arrival.

"I figured we could have some fun tonight," Bianca breathed. They had a brief—very brief—history together. She worked in banking, and they had met at a charity function. She was a beautiful woman he had wined and dined, then fucked.

But now, he was beyond irritated to have her in his apartment.

"And you thought to just drop by?"

Walking into his kitchen, he opened the drawer where he kept all his favorite takeout menus.

"Well, you didn't answer your phone."

She came to stand next to him, her hands sliding along his back as she leaned her face against his arm. Gently disengaging himself from her, he pulled out the menus for his favorite pizza joints.

"Maybe you should've gotten the hint that I didn't want to speak with you."

Walking past her, he looked down at his watch, wondering how much longer Alana would be.

"I just figured you were buried in work."

Her laugh was like nails on a chalkboard, causing him to grimace. He wasn't sure what he saw in her before.

Taking a seat on the couch, he spread the

menus out on the coffee table, trying to decide which restaurant he would order from.

"Working hard pays the bills," he muttered. He didn't need her reminding him of what his brother and family had been telling him for years.

"And it allows you to play hard."

She slid onto the couch next to him, her short skirt leaving little to the imagination. Her long legs were tan and golden, but didn't do anything for him.

He realized he preferred a deep caramel skinned woman. Almond-shaped eyes that were magnified by her quirky glasses. If he closed his eyes, he could still taste her from their kiss in the bookshop.

"I wasn't trying to go anywhere this weekend. I just wanted to relax at home for once."

"That's cool." Her hand rested on his knee, and instead of desire rushing through him, he only felt nauseous. She ran her hand up his leg and leaned into him with a small smile on her lips. "We can have plenty of fun here if you like. Anything you want to do, I'm down for it."

He just wanted her to leave.

Any other time, he would go with the flow of

having a beautiful woman show up at his apartment. He was always down for a little fun.

But now, there was only one person he wanted to spend time with.

Where was Alana?

He glanced down at his watch again.

"Seriously, you've looked at your watch at least three times since I've been here," Bianca whined.

"That's what happens when you show up uninvited," he snapped, getting to his feet.

"I just wanted us to have a little—"

"Us?" he growled, all patience gone. "There has never been an 'us.'"

"London!"

"We fucked. That was it. There was nothing between us, and there's not going to be. You were just an easy lay."

"Fuck you," Bianca screeched, her face contorted in anger as she stalked toward him. "You're a dick, you know that?"

"A dick you're not getting tonight," he snapped.

Her eyes flared. She looked as though she had more to say, but she spun around and stalked through the apartment toward the door.

"Your dick wasn't all that," she threw out over her shoulder.

"Yet here you are, showing up unannounced to my house, wanting me to fuck you."

A cynical laugh escaped him at the now comical situation. Bianca flipped him off before swinging open the door and disappearing out into the hall, leaving it wide open.

He walked over and watched her storm down the hallway toward the elevator. Shaking his head, he focused on the door across from his apartment.

Walking across the hall, he knocked on Alana's door. He cursed himself for spending so much time with her lately and not getting her cell phone number.

He listened at the door for any sounds of life.

Nothing.

He knocked again and waited. Most women he knew took forever getting ready. Maybe Alana was the same. It had been almost an hour since they had separated.

After no answer, he backed up and went inside his place.

What the hell?

Alana had appeared to be excited to come spend more time with him. Neither of them wanted the night to end.

What happened?

He'd never been known as a stalker, but now, London had perfected the art. He glanced out the peephole to see if he could catch a glimpse of Alana.

Not seeing any movement in the hall, he turned away from his door.

Is she avoiding me?

He wasn't sure what he had done for her to disappear and cut him out of her life that quick. Almost a week had gone by since their all-day outing, and all he could do was think about her. He couldn't get her out of his head.

The sound of her laughter. The way her eyes twinkled with mischief, and the way she moaned as they kissed.

Running a hand through his hair, he plopped down on the couch and snagged his laptop off the coffee table.

Today, he had decided to work from home, hoping to run into Alana. But somehow, she had managed to leave her apartment without him knowing it.

He just had to speak with her.

Maybe he would throw himself back into work. That always helped him feel better. Logging into the email system, he figured he'd start there and catch up.

A few minutes later, he leaned back and stared at the ceiling.

He couldn't concentrate.

Had he lost his touch?

Most women were all over him, but it would appear he was just another guy to Alana. In the day they had spent together, he took notice of everything about her. She was kind, polite to everyone who crossed their path, and was just downright different from any woman he had ever dated.

His phone rang. Leaning forward, he swiped it from the table.

"What?" he answered.

"Well, aren't you a ray of sunshine this morning."

Brad was one of the top agents who worked for Primetime Sports Management. He was a good guy and a talented agent who was known to cut jaw-dropping deals for his clients.

"Just tired. Been working since early this morning," London lied.

"Why am I not surprised? You own the company, and still put us all to shame with the hours you work."

"Hey, I have to be a role model for what I want in an employee," London snorted. He took pride in his position. When he and Jaxon first created the company, it was just the two of them, and they easily pulled in seventy hours a week. Now that PSM has been flourishing, he probably didn't need to work long hours, but he couldn't help it. That was just how he was programed. "Can't have you outshining me."

"I hear you're going to have a meeting with Khalil." Respect could be heard in Brad's voice.

"That's going to be record-breaking if you're able to sign him."

"Details haven't been worked out, but we're going to sit down, and I'll pitch to him why he should sign with me."

"You have something planned?"

"Yeah. I'm working on getting a deal with Cleveland. If he signs with me, I'll already have a sweet deal waiting for him," London bragged slightly. He had a great relationship with the Cleveland basketball program's front office. Over the past few years, he had begun a courtship of the legendary basketball player. They ran in the same circles and saw each other frequently. It was only a matter of time before the athlete would start thinking of signing with another sports agency.

"And I'm sure your percentage will cut you a nice piece."

"Of course. I'm worth it," London replied.

Setting his computer down on the couch, he rested his feet on the table and yawned, running a hand along the side of his face. His hand was met with hard bristles along his jaw. He hadn't shaved in a few days, and it was showing.

"So what's up? I doubt you're calling me on a Saturday to discuss work."

"Actually, I sort of am." Brad cleared his throat before continuing. "There's going to be a yacht party down on the lake tonight, and I wanted to extend an invite to you."

London thought about the offer. A month ago, he wouldn't have hesitated. Part of their job was to smooch up to clients and ensure they had everything they would need for them to sign a contract.

Now, partying on a yacht didn't sound too appealing to him.

"Do you need help pulling the client?"

If Brad needed him to help close the deal, then he would go. He and Jaxon were always supportive of their agents, and if they needed to be involved to ensure contracts were signed, they would be there. Their agents' success was theirs.

"Naw, I got it. Manny Lopez will be signing one of the biggest contracts in the baseball league thanks to me." Brad's voice was muffled while he spoke to someone next to him. "Anyway, I didn't know if you'd want to celebrate with us."

"I'm going to pass tonight."

It was out of the norm for him to turn down celebrating with clients of his company, but tonight, he didn't want to party. He wanted to spend time with a certain woman who was currently avoiding him.

"All right, man. See you Monday?"

"Yup. Have a great time. Make sure videos get recorded so marketing can put it out on social media."

Most of the younger athletes had a big presence on social media, and PSM had to have one too. He wanted to make sure his company stayed in sight of all athletes, especially ones that would be going pro.

"Will do."

Disconnecting the call, London tossed his phone on the cushion next to him. Running his hands over his face, his ears perked up at the faint sound of a conversation out in the hallway.

Bolting from the couch, he jogged over to door, ignoring how out of character this was for him.

London Keith never chased women.

But here he was, staring through the peephole.

"There you are," he muttered, seeing Alana sliding the key into her lock. Opening his door, he folded his arms in front of his chest.

Alana's eyes grew wide when they landed on him.

Damn, she was gorgeous.

Today she was dressed in dark jeans that

molded to her curves. A green T-shirt with a weird symbol on it, and matching green Chuck Taylor's on her feet.

Her hair was parted into two long ponytails. Her glasses were large and green.

He wasn't sure when it happened, but he loved the geeky girl look on her.

"Hello, Alana," he greeted her, forcing himself to stay calm.

"London." She hefted up the strap of her bag on her shoulder, her hand shaking slightly as she pushed her glasses higher on her nose. "How are you?"

"I'm not sure. I was supposed to have company over for dinner, but she never showed."

"Oh." She blinked, but didn't say anything else.

"What happened to you?"

"You looked occupied."

Alana seemed guarded, and he didn't like it. He needed to see her smiling and laughing.

"How would you know that?" he asked, confused. It was then he realized she must have seen Bianca go into his apartment. He looked between her door and his. "That wasn't what it looked like."

"London, who you entertain in your home is not my business."

She must have been looking through the peephole.

"Were you watching me?"

Her big brown eyes grew even wider.

"No. Okay, maybe."

He stalked across the hall until her back was pressed against the door.

"And how often have you watched me?"

She tilted her head back to meet his gaze. "Often."

A couple came around the corner, deep in a conversation. London recognized them as the neighbors at the end of the hall. The gentleman gave a nod, and London jerked his head in greeting. The woman's giggle floated through the air as they entered their condo.

Feeling Alana pressed up against him unleashed the beast inside of him. His cock strained against his sweats, demanding to be let out. Alana's supple breasts brushed against his chest. His gaze dropped to the base of her neck, watching her pulse skyrocket.

"When you were looking through your peephole, did you see that Bianca left not long after she arrived?"

He slid his hand around her waist, pulling her

close, ensuring nothing could get in between them.

She shook her head.

"She wasn't who I wanted to spend my evening with," he murmured.

"No?"

"I'd told you already what I wanted." Her nostrils flared. He knew she remembered what he'd said in the bookstore.

He dropped a hard kiss to her lips, the need to have her consuming him. Her whimper fed the fire burning inside of him.

"I've thought about nothing but you all week."

Another kiss.

Alana's chest was rising and falling rapidly.

He buried his face in the crook of her neck, the scent of her perfume filling his nostrils. Nipping her neck, he trailed his tongue up to her ear, taking it between his teeth.

"I need you, Alana. I want to thrust my cock inside your tight little cunt. Tonight."

Alana moaned, her hands gripping his shirt in a tight hold.

"London…"

He rested his hand on the door beside her head. Their lips connected again, and this time, she pushed her hips forward against him. Her mouth was hungry for his. His tongue stroked hers, allowing him to get a taste of her.

He'd missed this.

The feel of her soft, curvy body molding so perfectly against his. It was as if she were made for him.

"Do you want to feel me inside of you?"

"God, yes," she breathed.

"Then open the fucking door, Alana," he growled. "Unless you want our neighbors to watch me fuck you right here in the hallway."

Spinning around, she jiggled the key and unlocked the door. Pushing it open, she walked inside and turned, her focus on him.

He stalked through the entryway and shut the door behind him while Alana shrugged off her messenger bag, letting it fall to the floor. Moving to stand in front of her, he fought to keep his hands to himself.

"Second thoughts? Because now would be the time for you to tell me to go home."

er heart was racing away like a runaway train. She had tried her best to stay clear of London, not wanting to face him after last week. She had gotten her hopes up, and they had been crushed.

Stomped into the ground.

Alana didn't know how he knew what time she got home, but she hadn't expected for him to come flying out of his apartment and practically devour her with one kiss.

Her lips still tingled.

Lord. Have. Mercy.

That kiss practically took her breath away.

Made her forget why she was avoiding him.

Standing before him, she took him in. His hair was tussled, as if he had been running his hands through it. Her gaze wandered down to the tight fitted T-shirt that molded to his body. She knew from their conversations that he loved working out.

Through his gray sweat pants, she could see the silhouette of his hard cock pressing against the heavy cotton material.

From the size of his bulge, she knew he was working with something to brag about.

"Alana," London murmured, getting her attention. Smirking, he reached for her, his thumb running along her bottom lip. "What will it be? Am I staying or going home?"

"Stay," she replied, her voice ending in a squeak.

He bent down and captured her lips again, the kiss anything but gentle. Alana wrapped her arms around London's neck to hold on for dear life.

His lips moved along hers, tempting her, enticing her even more.

Her body trembled with need.

Had she gone into his apartment that night, she

knew she wouldn't have come home until the next morning.

Lifting her up into his arms, she wrapped her legs around his waist.

Without a word, he carried her into her bedroom.

Stopping beside her bed, he allowed her to slide down the length of him. Alana whimpered at the feeling of every inch of his hard muscles gliding against her body.

She wanted to see what he looked like beneath the clothing. Her hands were busy exploring the ridges of his abdomen when he tore his lips from hers.

"Undress," he ordered. The deep huskiness that accompanied his words made her eyes snap up to his.

His gray eyes were dark, almost black. That look, and the commanding tone in his voice, had her panties growing even more damp.

Her hands shook as she reached down and hooked her fingers underneath the edge of her shirt. Pulling it up and over her head, she tossed it to the floor.

London's gaze dropped to her taut nipples, straining against her bra.

The look in his eyes was downright feral.

"Keep going."

Alana grew bolder. Kicking off her shoes, she reached for the button of her jeans and unsnapped them. Undoing the zipper, she shimmied them down her legs and kicked them off to the side.

Her heart raced at the pure hunger that consumed London's expression.

He stood there, his arms folded in front of him. It didn't go unnoticed that his hands were balled into fists.

Holding his gaze, she reached around and undid her bra. Next, she eased her panties down her legs.

The sound of London's quick intake of breath made her shudder.

"Fuck, you're beautiful."

Closing the space between them, he reached for her.

"Nope," Alana objected, sidestepping him. If she had to be naked, so did he. She motioned to his clothes, wanting to see if her fantasy lived up to reality. "Strip."

"Fine."

With a cocky grin, he pulled off his shirt. She took a moment to appreciate the well-defined ridges of his abdomen, her tongue aching to trace each of them. She made a promise to herself that later, she would do just that.

His pants were next to go, along with his shoes. His cotton boxer briefs did nothing to hide the massive erection pushing against them.

Once the briefs joined his clothes on the floor, all joking was put aside.

Alana couldn't take her eyes off the massive cock that hung between London's legs.

Her fantasy couldn't live up to the real thing. London was a gorgeous specimen of a man, his cock standing proudly erect.

Her heart fluttered in anticipation of what was to come.

"Is that better?" he asked, closing the distance between them once more.

"Yes."

Gently removing her glasses, he sat them down on the nightstand.

Alana whimpered at the feeling of his warm skin against hers. London moved his hand to the base of her neck and slid his fingers into her hair, pulling her head back so she was looking up at him.

London covered her mouth with his while forcing her toward the bed. She soon found herself on her back with London hovering over her. Breaking the kiss, he braced his hands on either side of her head against the mattress.

His lips burned a fiery trail along her jawline. He buried his face in the crook of her neck, pressing open kisses to her sensitive skin.

Her hands were on an exploration of their own. She caressed his shoulders and ran her hands down his back.

His heavy cock rested along her inner thigh. She ached to have it plunge deep inside of her.

That would come soon enough.

London continued to lick and nip her skin as he worked his way down. When his mouth closed around her nipple, she gasped.

Closing her eyes, she basked in the sensation of him rolling her nipple around with his tongue, worshiping her breast before moving to the other one.

Her back arched off the bed as heat and fire raced through her.

London continued to tease and torment her while moving farther down her body. Her fingers threaded into his thick hair as his head dipped lower on her body.

Shifting, Alana opened for him, her core clenched with need. Desire coiled in her belly for this man.

No longer was she thinking of anything else but the moment they were in.

She was going to hold on to it for as long as she could.

One night.

She would give herself to him, then deal with the consequences in the morning.

He found her clit without hesitation. Her back again arched off the bed as he licked and sucked her sensitive nub. His tongue was magical while stroking and licking all of her.

Whimpers and cries escaped Alana's lips, as if she were possessed. She had never responded to a man like this before.

London knew all the right buttons to push. She was writhing on the bed in a heightened state of arousal.

It was as if she was having an out-of-body experience, watching herself be devoured by the sexiest man alive.

She didn't recognize any of the sounds spilling

from her lips as London drove her higher and higher to the stars.

He slid a finger inside of her.

"So fucking tight."

Her pussy clenched tight around his digit. She was close to climaxing, and would welcome the wave of sensations.

Alana opened her mouth to speak, but the words that came out were incomprehensible.

He added another finger, stretching her even more.

He finger fucked her slowly while sucking her clit. She had never had a lover who was so intent on ensuring she was satisfied, offering such intense pleasure.

Her eyes pressed closed as the moans continued to pour from her. Her fingers gripped his hair while riding his face and hands.

"London…"

Her muscles tensed and her body shook as her orgasm hit.

As the aftershocks rippled their way through every nerve in her body, she closed her eyes, trying to catch her breath.

The bed shifted as London crawled over her.

"Open your eyes," he commanded.

When she did, they met his lust-filled ones.

Pushing her thighs wider, he gripped the base of his cock and guided it to her entrance.

Her breath caught in her throat at the sensation of the tip pushing its way inside.

It was a snug fit, and Alana nearly panicked, remembering the size of his member.

What if he doesn't fit?

It was a silly thought, but none of the men she had been with before were as big as London.

"Fuck," he hissed as he slowly pushed his way inside of her.

"Oh God," she groaned when she felt herself stretch to accommodate him.

Covering her mouth with his, she became lost in the kiss, his tongue stroking hers, engaging hers to play. Relaxing, she returned the kiss with the same fervor.

Alana forgot to breathe as he settled completely inside of her.

"Breathe, Alana," he murmured, kissing the corner of her mouth. She inhaled sharply, then blew out through her mouth.

He withdrew slightly before thrusting forward. Her pussy grew impossibly slick while stretching to take his full girth.

"Atta girl."

Opening her eyes, she held his gaze while he repeated the motion.

"Yes," she hissed through clenched teeth. Gripping her thigh, he raised it higher, opening her even more to him.

He began moving faster, and she felt the stirrings of another orgasm racing through her.

How can that be?

Two orgasms back-to-back? With Danny, she would be so lucky if he gave her an orgasm. Any of her good ones came as the result of her own hand.

Alana began to move her hips, meeting him thrust for thrust. His gentleness soon faded, and he pumped hard, filling her to the hilt.

"London," she cried out, her arms wrapped around his shoulders, needing him closer.

His breaths were coming fast as he took everything he wanted, and everything she desired to give him.

"Alana" he growled. Each time he slammed into her, it pushed her closer to climax. His long shaft hit every nerve inside of her. "You feel so good around my dick."

Alana's breath hitched in her throat as he

continued to pound into her. She no longer recognized the voice chanting London's name.

Her nails dug into his arms, her muscles growing taut. She was on the brink of euphoria.

London grunted, shifting his hips mid-stride, causing him to rub her clit with each thrust.

Alana shattered, screaming London's name.

He thrust harder until a shudder ripped through him. The muscles underneath her hands grew tight as he finally reached his climax, bellowing her name.

She was absolutely beautiful. Her smooth brown skin was flawless and was as soft as he had imagined.

London continued to watch Alana while she slept.

She snuggled closer to him automatically in her sleep. For some strange reason, he loved that she appeared to seek him out while she slept.

His cock stiffened, as if knowing the curvy woman who had caught his eye was close. He shouldn't be able to even get hard.

He'd taken her countless times last night, his

appetite for her only slightly quenched. Glancing at the clock on the nightstand, he saw it had only been about two hours since she'd fallen asleep.

London had only dozed for a short while.

He couldn't stop thinking of their night, the sex between them explosive.

Addictive.

He couldn't get enough.

For the first time in his life, London didn't want to leave a woman before she woke up. He wanted to be the first person Alana saw when she opened her eyes.

Just that fast, he knew he had feelings for her. He wasn't familiar with them, but he knew she was special to him.

Unable to stop himself from touching her, he reached up and gently brushed her hair away from her face. Her pigtails were long gone, and her dark strands were spread along his arm and across the pillows.

She looked so peaceful.

Waking up with Alana in his arms had him feeling content with life.

Alana shifted on the bed, grumbling under her breath. Her feet moved, sliding along his calves.

A moan slipped from her lips as she slowly began to wake. After a few blinks, she met his gaze.

"Morning."

Her lips curved into a smile, her shy veil sliding into place.

"Morning."

She had a sexy huskiness to her voice that shot a bolt of electricity straight to his dick. Her gaze darted from the door and back to him. He sensed she had a burning question.

"What's wrong?" he asked, entwining their fingers together. Placing a kiss to the back of her hand, he settled it against his chest.

Biting her lip, she stared at him, deep in thought. It was cute, but he wanted to know what the problem was.

"Well, don't you usually have girls leave before morning? At least it would seem that—"

"Wait, what?" He grew still. How did she know women left his house before morning? "Were you stalking me?"

He wasn't angry. He was just going to make her suffer a little before putting her out of her misery.

But she was correct.

He never allowed women to stay for breakfast.

He didn't want them growing attachments to him. It was only fun—no strings.

Now, with Alana, he wanted the strings—deep connections and promises.

She flinched. Sitting up and resting on her elbow, he watched the sheet slide down, exposing the swell of her breasts.

Breasts he had come to know intimately. He had memorized every inch of her throughout the night, tasted every part of her. He grew hard thinking of doing it all over again. The sounds of her sighs, gasps, and moans still echoed in his mind.

"Not that I meant to. It was just fascinating to watch—"

"Fascinating?"

What was so compelling about women leaving his apartment?

"I'm just curious by nature. Forget I said anything."

Closing her eyes, she fell back against the pillows. She tried to yank the blanket over her face, but he held onto it.

"Oh, no. I want to know what was going through that beautiful brain of yours as you were watching my apartment," he chuckled. A short game of tug of war commenced, with Alana losing.

London tossed the blanket off the bed and onto the floor.

"Hey!" Alana shrieked. He gathered her to him as she tried to struggle, but it died off soon as her naked body pressed against his. "You don't fight fair."

"I'm a man who goes after who and what he wants," he stated, pressing his lips to hers.

She instantly softened, allowing him to have his way with her. The kiss sent a blaze of fire through him. Molding herself to him, she drew him close, and he soon found himself on top of her, sliding into her.

They both moaned in unison.

"I can't get enough of you," he admitted, nipping her ear with his teeth as his hips set a slow rhythm. Wanting to see her face as she climaxed, he sat up and wrapped her thighs around his hips. "Spend the weekend with me."

"Okay."

She was right.

He didn't play fair.

This was the most time he had spent with a woman not related to him. He couldn't even remember if he had ever spent a day with a woman, much less an entire weekend.

Alana sat on the couch with her feet tucked under her. She was dressed in a long sleep shirt with Captain America's shield on it. He laughed at the wording.

Cap's Girl.

He wasn't sure if she realized how cute she was when she was lost in her thoughts. She unconsciously nibbled on her lower lip, while her glasses slid down dangerously to the tip of her nose.

She automatically pushed them up and back into place. As if sensing him looking at her, she turned and focused her big brown eyes on him.

"What? Do I have something on my face?" She gave a slow blink and felt along her cheeks.

He smiled at her. "Not at all."

She gave him a weird look before going back to reading whatever was on her screen.

Sighing, he put his feet up on the coffee table.

This seemed right.

He didn't know what it was, but just being around Alana was all he needed.

He looked down at his laptop screen, but he

didn't see any of the numbers or statistics that were spread out before him. Closing his laptop, he set it down on the table, pushed up from the chair, and moved over to the couch next to Alana.

"Do you usually work on Sundays?"

"Not usually, but one of my coworkers is out on vacation and I'm covering for them."

Yesterday, they had spent the entire day in bed. Gazing over at the dark mark on Alana's neck, he felt his cock jerk.

That was his mark on her, and it did something to him. It was like an animalistic triumph claiming her as his. Reaching over, he closed her computer and pulled her onto his lap so she straddled him. He pulled her close, bringing the warmth of her core against him.

His cock jerked at the feeling of her on top of him.

"What are you doing?" she giggled, wrapping her arms around him while staring into his eyes.

"I think we both need to relax and take the day off."

Holy hell. He couldn't believe he was saying this. London was a workaholic, and he played hard too. But today, he just wanted to spend time with Alana.

"What do you have in mind?"

His first thought was to pick her up and carry her back into the bedroom. They would have plenty of time for that if he had his way.

"Sailing? I have a small boat we can take out on the lake," he suggested.

"Really? As long as I've lived here, I've never been out on the lake."

"Then it's settled. I'll run over to my apartment, get dressed, and meet you back here."

"I don't know," she purred, her hands sliding through his hair, sending a jolt of desire straight through him. "Last time you went to your apartment alone, a random woman showed up."

London's mouth dropped open in shock.

His sexy geek had jokes.

"Seriously?" he scoffed.

Grabbing her by the waist, he tickled her. Her screams pierced the air as laughter flowed out of her. She jerked and moved around, trying to free herself from his hold.

Jerking and moving around to free herself from his hold, her shirt rode up along her waist, revealing she had only a pair of panties on beneath it. His cock was fully engorged.

"Uncle!" she hollered, tears flowing down her

face as she tried to catch her breath. "I was just playing!"

"You're going to pay for that."

He could take a good joke as well as the next man, but at the moment, he didn't want to think of any other woman but the sexy, curvy one on his lap.

Skating his hand along her thigh, he slipped his fingers underneath her panties and pushed them to the side. Her breath caught in her throat as he parted her labia and found her swollen nub.

"London," she whimpered.

He bit his lip, focusing on her face. She closed her eyes and moaned when he strummed her little bundle of nerves. Her hands rested on his shoulders, her nails digging into his bare shoulders as she gyrated against his hand.

"Do you think I'm thinking of any other woman right now?" he questioned, needing to make sure she had no doubts. The little comments she had made since they'd met had stayed in the back of his mind. She thought she knew him, but Alana had yet to reach the core of who he was.

"No."

He dipped his finger into her pussy, finding her drenched.

"Alana, take me out of my sweats."

Her eyes fluttered opened. There was a slightly dazed look in them, but it cleared up after she blinked several times. Reaching down, she loosened his pants and reached her small hand inside.

He groaned when her fingers wrapped around his stiff member and guided him out. They both worked his pants down to fully free him.

"Slide down on me." He kept her panties pushed to the side, impatient to feel her surround him. Lifting up, she slid down his shaft, slowly. London's breath caught in his throat as her warm, slick core enveloped him.

She was so damn tight.

Sweat broke out along his forehead.

Once she was seated fully, he tugged her sleeping shirt over her head and tossed it to the side.

The plans for sailing could wait.

"Ride me," he growled. Alana's hips rotated around in a circle, almost sending him over the edge. Fuck, he was wound up tight for her.

The sight of her pretty brown mounds swayed in front of him. He reached up and captured one of her nipples with his lips, her skin soft and sweet. His tongue rolled her beaded bud, teasing it.

"London," she groaned, her fingers threading into his hair as she held on.

Their movements quickened. London lifted her up and down while he thrust his hips upward, forcing himself deeper.

"Fuck," he bit out, his lips brushing against her breasts.

Their eyes connected, and London was lost in her beautiful brown orbs. He didn't want to be anywhere else but deep inside of Alana. He didn't want anyone else. She was perfect for him.

The sound of their lovemaking filled the air. Alana's moans, his grunts, and their heavy breathing was all he wanted to hear. It fueled him on. Her core was magical, and he had to fight to keep from releasing too soon.

Not without Alana.

Pulling her forward, he worked her body at a different angle. She stiffened, giving in to her climax.

It was his name on her lips as she crested. He could no longer hold off and joined her, emptying himself into her.

Alana gasped, taking in the open waters surrounding them. "London, this is breathtaking." His small yacht was luxurious, which did not surprise her.

London never half-assed anything.

The salon part of the boat had a galley, a television, microwave and fridge. It had plenty of seating areas, and everything needed to entertain.

London sat in the helm's seat and operated the boat, the epitome of sexiness. He was dressed in shorts, a T-shirt, and wore a pair of dark aviator sunglasses. He looked so relaxed behind the controls of the boat.

The salon allowed them to see everything. The glass windows and sunroof were for the sunlight to enter. From her seat, she could watch the other boats sailing by.

Reaching over, he flipped a switch that opened the sunroof.

"This is amazing. Do you come out here often?" she asked.

"As much as I can. I've sailed to Canada, Michigan, and Pennsylvania on these waters. It's a great way to escape."

When they had arrived, he had given her a full tour. The lower level—or the stateroom, as he had called it—housed a bedroom, a bathroom with a shower, and even a small lounge.

Alana had to admit, she was definitely impressed. She knew he and his company were doing well, but this just proved it.

The weather was perfect, and the day was turning into a lazy Sunday.

Her thoughts went back to that morning in her living room.

The sex between them had been explosive.

Something changed between them. Alana wasn't sure what it was, but she could definitely feel it.

"What are you thinking about?"

"How you're spoiling me."

Smiling, he waved her over to him.

"Come learn to sail." He patted his lap for her to sit on.

She giggled, and did as she was told. His muscular arms encircled her, guiding her hands onto the steering wheel.

"Are you sure?" She grew nervous. Somehow, she felt that driving a boat differed greatly from a car. "What if I hit something? I don't want to damage your boat."

"Guide the wheel. There's nothing close enough for you to run into."

Taking a deep breath, she held onto the wheel.

It wasn't bad. Actually, it was easy.

"I'm really driving?" she asked.

"You sure are."

"But how do I know where we're going?"

Making some adjustments, he replied, "Let me worry about that."

"So where are we going?"

"Put-in-Bay. We can grab something to eat there."

"I've never been."

"How have you lived in Ohio this long and never been on Lake Erie or Put-in-Bay?

"I don't know."

It was then she realized she may have led a sheltered life.

"Well, it's a good thing you've got me."

Her core clenched at the heated look he gave her.

Down, girl, she chided herself.

Her libido was out of control. A weekend filled with hot, sweaty sex, and her body was trying to make sure she was always ready.

"Don't look at me like that, Alana."

"Like what?"

She couldn't help her curious nature. How was she looking at him?

"Your eyes are telling me you want my cock buried deep inside you again."

Kissing her cheek, he then moved to her ear, his teeth snagging her earlobe. His warm breath caressed her skin, sending a shiver of desire coursing through her.

It was astounding how her body reacted to his. London Keith could do whatever he wanted to her.

"London," she breathed, her eyes fluttering

closed. They quickly snapped back open, as she almost forgot she was driving the boat. Lucky for her, there was nothing but open waters.

"What is it?"

His hands slipped underneath her shirt, gliding across her belly.

"There's something else I haven't done before," she confessed as he fondled her breasts.

"And that is?"

"I've never had sex on a boat in open water."

The growl that came out of his mouth was something she'd never heard before.

"Go down to the stateroom, Alana." Helping her off his lap, he pushed those sexy aviator glasses up to the top of his head, giving her an intense glare. Her breath froze in her chest. Standing, he hit a few buttons on the control panel. "When I get down there, you better be naked and waiting on the bed."

Alana turned and sped down the stairs, not needing to be told twice.

London's breath tickled her ear.

"Good morning."

Alana groaned and snuggled closer to him. His warm body was heaven. She didn't want to leave the cocoon of his arms.

It was Monday morning, and time for reality to set it.

Her sex filled weekend with the hottest guy she'd ever met was over.

"Five more minutes."

"Nope. Time to get up."

Flinging the covers off of her, she shrieked as the cool air of the room kissed her bare skin.

"What are you doing?" she groaned, catching him staring at her with a wide grin.

"Someone not a morning person?"

Removing his arm from under her, he rolled out of bed. The sight of his naked form had her reaching for her glasses.

His body was perfection.

"I'm not a Monday morning person," she replied through a yawn.

Propping her head up on a pillow, she watched him walk around the bed, taking in the sight of his semi-hard cock.

Now that was something she'd wake up bright and early for on a Monday.

"Come on, Alana."

Coming to her side of the bed, he captured her ankle in his hand.

"What? Wait a minute!" she yelped as he dragged her to the edge. She didn't even look at the alarm clock on her nightstand. One peek at the window revealed the sun wasn't even up yet.

What time was it?

He pulled her to the edge and lifted her up into his arms. She playfully wiggled around, trying to get out of his grasp. Laughing at her antics, he tightened his hold on her.

"We're going to take a shower together so we can get ready for work."

Stopping her thrashing, she settled in against him.

A shower?

"Oh, okay."

Easing her down his body once they were in the bathroom, she whimpered at the feeling of his hard cock brushing her stomach. With a smirk, London turned and started the shower.

She reached for her shower cap and put it on her head to protect her hair. It was leopard print, and it was adorable.

"Come on in. The water's fine."

Stepping inside, he positioned her in front of

him so she was under the warm spray. The temperature was perfect.

"Do we have to go to work?" she whined.

"Yes, we do." Laughing, he reached for her loofa. "What are you wanting to do? Stay in bed for all eternity and only come out for food and water?"

"It's a thought," she huffed, imagining such a fantasy. It would be divine. She giggled, and the giggle morphed into a full-blown belly laugh.

"Silly Alana. As much as I would love to keep you in bed forever, we have to make a living."

Alana fell silent as he began to wash her. She'd never had anyone take care of her like this.

"You do know I'm capable of doing this."

"I know, but I want to do it."

His gaze flickered to hers before turning back to his activity. He moved over her breasts, cleaning them well before going lower. He cleaned her belly before motioning for her to spin around.

She turned away from him, marveling at how good it felt to have his hands on her. She bit back a moan as his other hand rested on her waist.

Closing her eyes, she tried to beat down the fear that this would be the last time they'd be together. London didn't normally date the same woman, and it was out of the norm for him to spend an entire weekend with one.

She would hold on to the memories they had made together.

She hadn't really been on the dating scene before falling into bed with him, and didn't have any urge to do so now.

How could she?

After the weekend they had shared, how could she move on?

They quickly finished their shower and made their way into her bedroom. She averted his eyes when he unwrapped the towel from around his waist. It would be torture knowing this would probably be the last time she saw it.

She pulled on her robe while he dressed in the sweats and T-shirt he had worn in her apartment.

Alana wasn't quite sure what to say. Their time together was officially coming to an end.

"I better go. I don't want to make you late to work," London said.

"I'll walk you to the door."

Tightening the belt on her robe, she followed behind him as he gathered his things. She felt a moment of sadness. Just that quick, she had gotten used to him in her place.

Arriving at the door, he opened it and turned to her.

"Have a great day at work."

He used his free hand to tilt her chin up. Her breath caught in her throat as he bent down and pressed his lips to hers. It was the softest kiss she'd ever experienced. She stepped closer, closing the gap between them. Lifting his head, he stared into her eyes. "See you later?"

Unable to speak, she jerked her head in a nod.

"Lock up behind me." He swiped his thumb slowly across her bottom lip before releasing her.

Alana leaned against her doorjamb, watching him unlock his door. When it opened, he glanced at her over his shoulder and tossed her a wink before going inside.

She had secretly wished for a night with Mr. Hotness. Well, she got it, and a whole lot more.

Now she was going to have to step back into reality.

Chapter Thirteen

"How is it I haven't heard from you all weekend?" Sofie asked.

Alana took a sip of her Coke and shrugged. Normally, they would talk on the phone or hang out. This was the first weekend they had done neither.

Work had been hard, as Alana could barely concentrate. All she could think about was a tall, handsome man with the clearest gray eyes who had fucked her into oblivion.

Picking up her fork, she dove into her food. When Sofie had called and invited her out to lunch, she practically ran from her office. She had wasted her day away, caught up in all her memories.

"I was actually busy this weekend."

Sofie narrowed her eyes, her suspicion making Alana feel guilty.

"Doing what?"

It wasn't like she could've called her bestie in the middle of back-to-back orgasms. That would've been cruel.

Moans and screams were all that would have poured from Alana's mouth.

Nope.

She chose to wait until she could see her friend in person, to tell her what all she'd been up to. Not that Alana was the type to kiss and tell, but there were some things a girl had to share with her bestie.

"Let's just say the dry spell is over," Alana whispered, keeping her eyes on her plate when Sofie shrieked.

"Are you kidding me?" she cried, bursting into laughter. Alana tried to keep from smiling, but lost the battle. Grinning, she danced in her seat while Sofie dabbed at the corners of her eyes. "Okay, that was not what I was expecting. He kept you occupied the entire weekend? Who was the lucky guy, and you better not tell me it was Danny."

Alana snorted. There was no way in hell she'd be this happy about having sex with Danny. That man was no longer in her memories after her weekend with London.

"Nope. Not Danny."

"Look at your face. That's the expression of someone who was dickmatized," Sofie giggled at her own joke. "Don't leave me in the dark. Who was it?"

Alana took another sip of her drink, trying to buy some time, but Sofie's wide eyes and foot tapping under their table wasn't going to allow her to wait any longer.

"It was Mr. Hotness."

Sofie froze. The woman didn't bat an eye or breathe. Had they been on the phone, Alana would've checked to see if the line had been disconnected.

"Earth to Sofie."

Blinking, Sofie leaned back in her chair.

"Did you say Mr. Hotness? The guy who lives across the hall from you?"

"I did. London and I—"

"London?" Sofie crowed. "I guess you and Mr. Hotness are now on a first name basis?"

Of course her friend would tease her.

"I mean, after the things that man did to me…"

"Okay. He must give good dick if he's got you looking like that."

"Sofie!" Alana looked around with wide eyes, praying no one around them heard her friend. The restaurant was busy with the lunch crowd, but everyone seemed to be ignoring the two of them.

"What?" Reaching for her drink, she took a sip and winked at Alana over her glass. "So was he any good?"

Alana knew what her friend was fishing for, but she didn't want to share the intimate details of what passed between London and her.

"London's actually a great guy."

The time they had spent together had allowed her to get to know the real London. He was open with her, playful and sweet.

The sex.

Dammit, it was going to take a while for her to forget that.

"Is that so? And him being such a great person has put that dreamy lovesick look in your eyes?"

"What are you talking about? We had fun. And believe it or not, we actually left my apartment too."

"How did you two hook up, anyway?"

Alana went into the entire story of her

returning home from running with Sofie and their meeting. Sofie listened, entranced by the story. Finally, she shared with Sofie their morning together and their goodbye.

"That's it?" Sofie exclaimed. "Just a see you later and have a great day at work?"

"I guess. I didn't want to seem like a clingy woman. I knew what I was getting into." Alana finished her meal and sat back. The waitress stopped by their table to check on them before leaving their check. "One night turned into a weekend."

" You said he never has the same woman over."

"I did." Alana's stomach clenched at Sofie's words. She was now officially a notch in his belt, along with all the other women who paraded into his life. She hadn't even thought about what their relationship would be like now that they'd had sex.

Would she see him in the hall and wave as he walked past with another woman?

Her heart rate spiked at the thought.

She didn't know if she could go through seeing countless women go in and out of his apartment.

"Are you all right, Alana?"

Blinking, she offered Sofie a smile, trying to play it cool. "Yeah, I am."

Sofie didn't look convinced.

"I'll be fine. People have one-night stands all the time. I got a weekend."

London knew Alana's routine. From his short stint as a stalker, he knew what time she would arrive home. On his way home from the office, he had picked up a large pizza.

Glancing down at his watch, he saw it was time for his girl.

When did she become his girl?

The second he took her out on his private boat.

He'd never taken a woman who wasn't related to him out on Lake Erie, particularly on his boat. Yes, his company owned a yacht for entertaining, but that was for business.

London jogged into his kitchen and took the pizza box out. Snatching his keys and phone from the counter, and headed out into the hallway, wanting to surprise Alana with dinner when she arrived home.

Stepping out into the hallway, he shut his door and waited. Within minutes, he heard the ding of the elevator stopping on their floor.

Moments later, he was rewarded with the sight of Alana walking toward her apartment.

"Welcome home."

He grinned at her shocked expression.

"What are you doing out here?" she asked as she drew closer. Today she was sporting a pair of oversized black-rimmed glasses, her hair pulled back into a low ponytail. She was dressed in a cheetah print blouse and black skirt, with matching cheetah Chucks.

Alana was the most beautiful woman he had ever seen. Her sense of style fit her. She was different from anyone he'd ever been with, and that was probably why he was drawn to her.

His entire day at work was wasted because he couldn't stop thinking about her.

He'd always had a rule of one night with women, but when it came to Alana, one night wasn't enough.

"I did promise you pizza." He motioned to the box he was carrying. "I was hungry when I left work and figured I'd pick up a bite to eat for the both of us."

"That's sweet of you."

She pushed up the large frames that had slid

down to the tip of her nose. When she pushed them up higher, London knew he was a goner.

He didn't want anyone but her.

"I guess that means tomorrow, dinner will be on me?" Her perfectly sculpted eyebrows rose at the question.

"I look forward to what you come up with."

Resting the box against his waist, he closed the gap between them and tilted her chin up so their eyes could meet. Unable to resist, he swooped down and captured her lips with his. He'd been waiting to feel her soft, plump lips against his all day.

It had taken all his control that morning to keep from having his way with her in the shower. Had he slid inside of her, they would have either been late for work, or taken the entire day off.

"Pepperoni pizza?" He nodded. "Good. That's my favorite. It'll go well with the wine I put in the fridge before I went to work this morning."

Unlocking the door, he followed her inside.

It had been six weeks since that first weekend she'd spent with London. It was late, and tonight they were staying in London's apartment. He was working on some major deal, and was preoccupied with work.

She was relaxing on the couch while he talked on the phone at the dining room table, running his fingers through his hair for the millionth time. His thick strands stood on end, and she smiled at how cute he looked.

Taking in his apartment, she remembered the first time he'd invited her to spend the night.

She'd refused, of course. She wasn't going to step one foot into his bedroom until he disinfected it. The memory of his face when she'd put in her request still made her smile. But she had been dead serious.

The number of women he'd had in there before her had her damn near throwing out the mattress.

But he'd done as she wished. He had a company come out to steam clean it, and had purchased all new bedding.

"If it takes all night, I'll close this," London growled into the phone.

Checking her watch, she saw it was close to ten. She was trying to stay awake, but her body was in the process of shutting down.

Pushing off the couch, she walked over to him just as he hung up the phone. Inhaling deeply, he cradled his head in his hands and blew it out slowly.

Rubbing his shoulders, she kissed the top of his head.

"Gonna be a long night?"

"God, yes." Turning, he wrapped his arms around her waist, resting his head against her chest. "Why don't you head to bed? I saw you yawn at least five times in the last two minutes."

"It wasn't five times," she chuckled.

"Okay, maybe ten," he joked.

When he looked up at her, she took notice of his bloodshot eyes and his five o'clock shadow.

"You sure you don't want to join me?"

"As tempting as that sounds, I can't."

Sitting back in his chair, he stared at his laptop. Taking advantage of the move, she slid onto his lap. Chuckling, he wrapped his arms around her.

"What could you possibly be getting done at this time of night?"

"Right now, I'm negotiating a contract for Khalil. If I can get him to sign with me, I'll get him the biggest deal ever made."

His eyes grew wide with excitement.

"What kind of money are we talking?" she inquired, running her fingers through his thick strands.

"Two hundred and seventy million dollars over five years."

Alana's hand froze. She knew he dealt with professional sports stars, and she'd heard of Khalil Roads. It wasn't like she lived under a rock.

But if Khalil signed a contract worth that amount, how much did London get?

"Oh my goodness," she breathed. "He'd be a fool not to sign with you."

Self-doubt really began to set in. What was he doing with a woman like her? Yes, she could afford her very expensive apartment, but that was thanks to the inheritance she received from her parents' deaths. She was just a regular woman who worked a day job, loved wine, board games, and hanging with her bestie.

"What's wrong? Where did you go?" London squeezed her side, gaining her attention.

"That's a shit ton of money."

"I know, and it'll look good for my agency. It'll show how hard we work for our clients, and everyone will want to sign. Khalil would be my focus. Some smaller athletes can work with one of the other agents, but I charge the big bucks."

She mustered up a smile, trying to push down the thoughts and emotions swirling around inside of her.

"That's amazing, London."

She knew their relationship would come to an end eventually. She wasn't the type of woman he had paraded around before. She wasn't the type to go out and party until the wee hours of the morning.

That wasn't her.

Alana had to face the reality that soon, what

they had would be over. He would tire of the short, thick, geeky girl. They were complete opposites.

She was just going to have to enjoy the moment. When she first slept with him, she had already decided it was what it was.

But she never would've guessed they would be still seeing each other.

She didn't even know if they had a name for what was happening between them.

Did she want to build more with him? Of course she did, but she didn't know if he felt the same.

What could she bring to the table? Here he was, swinging multimillion dollar deals, and she was just a financial analyst for an insurance company.

Pulling her close, he kissed her lips. "I have an idea."

"What's that?"

"Why don't you come with me to meet Khalil?"

Alana's eyes widened.

Go with him to meet a major NBA star?

"Me? Go with you?"

"Yes. Why are you surprised that I would ask you to be my date?"

She shrugged. They hadn't really gone out on official dates. They'd grabbed something to eat here and there, hit up her favorite bookstore and record shop.

She was content with what they had.

Deciding to just ask the question that had been burning inside of her for a while now, she blurted out, "Why me?"

"Why you what?"

London was confused. What was Alana asking him?

She bit her lip in that sexy way that drove him crazy.

"Why me? We've been together for a little bit now. I'm nothing like the women you were dating before—"

"I'm going to stop you now. I wasn't dating any of those women."

"You know what I mean." She motioned to her body. "I don't look like any of them."

"What the hell are you talking about?"

He was growing angry at what she was insinuating. Did she not know how beautiful she was? How much he loved her curves?

Getting up off his lap, she folded her arms over her chest.

"London, what are we doing, because I don't even know? Are we friends with benefits? Neighbors who have a little fun?"

London knew he was to blame for her confusion. Standing in front of her, he tilted her chin up so she could meet his gaze.

"Is that what you think this is between us? Friends who fuck?"

"I mean, I'm fine with what we have. I like hanging out with you—"

"Are you trying to say I should take someone else with me to meet Khalil?" he growled, his grip on her chin tightening.

"I mean, if—"

"Don't you dare say any crazy shit, Alana," he bit out. "If you haven't noticed, I love the way you look. These curves of yours are sexy as fuck." He ran his hands along her torso, stopping at her waist. He had gotten to know her body just as well as he knew his own.

He knew what made her moan, what made her gasp, and what she sounded like coming on his cock.

She was out of her damned mind if she thought

he wanted someone else. He'd had no desire to be with any other woman since meeting her.

Everything about her drew him to her.

Her smile. Her personality. Her quirkiness.

She was everything he wanted.

"I don't want anyone else to go with me. I want you by my side." Easing her stance, she laid her forehead against his chest, allowing him to hold her. "I enjoy spending time with you. If you want me to take you out to expensive restaurants and out on the town just so you know how much I like spending time with you, then that's what I'll do."

He had been content to do all the things she wanted to do. He was getting to an age where partying all night was getting old.

Now that he had someone to occupy his evenings, he'd rather be with her than out in the streets.

"I don't need that," she mumbled into his chest.

"I don't either. What we've had has been perfect. But wining and dining clients is part of my job." He gently lifted her chin so he could look into her eyes. "I would love to have you on my arm. Please say yes."

"Okay."

"Yeah?"

"Yes," she groaned, rolling those pretty brown eyes of hers, a smile appearing on her lips before a yawn replaced it.

"Not only are you going to have fun, you'll get to see me work my magic." Hugging her tight, he whispered against her hair, "Let's get you to bed."

He started leading her toward his bedroom.

"But what about work?" she protested.

"I have more pressing things to take care of at the moment," he replied, his hand sliding down to the curve of her ass.

He was going to show his woman how much he appreciated all her curves.

Chapter Fifteen

"London, you've been holding out," Khalil Roads declared with a laugh.

London winked at her. "She's a gem."

Alana felt her face warm at the compliment. Dinner with the NBA star was going well. She didn't know what to expect when meeting him, but finding out they shared a love for certain comic book movies was a plus.

"I just got London to start watching all the movies with me," she announced proudly.

"In order of release or chronological order?" Khalil asked, glancing at London.

She laughed at the pained look on London's face. He had been a good sport watching the movies with her. They had made their way to the first Thor movie, and he appeared to be enjoying them.

"We've been watching them in order of release."

Alana was enjoying herself. Finishing off her glass of wine, a waiter arrived at her side with another. They were at a fancy restaurant located in downtown Cleveland, one she had never been brave enough to go to.

It was so expensive, they didn't put prices on the menu.

"So tell me, Khalil. What are you looking for in an agent?" she inquired.

Did she really just ask him that?

It had to be the wine.

Khalil burst out laughing. She laughed as well, hoping she wasn't too forward with him.

Khalil wagged a finger at her. "I really do like her."

"Being curious by nature, I was just wondering. I'm a financial analyst, and in my line of work, I have to decide if my company would be taking risks on certain ventures."

She was good at what she did, and she hoped to

be up for a promotion soon. Her goal was to become lead analyst.

"Is that so?" Khalil's smile faded as he looked between London and her. "What are things you would look for if you were in my shoes?"

"Being wined and dined doesn't matter. You can afford to pay for this place yourself," she began. Khalil had been a professional athlete for a few years now and had made a buttload of money. "What you should do is analyze the past results of the agency trying to recruit you. What are your long-term goals? Can they meet them? Does their drive meet yours?"

Khalil grew silent.

He stared at Alana so long, she grew nervous, wondering if she had just ruined London's chances of signing him.

"You must do well at your job," Khalil pointed out.

At London's nod, she breathed a sigh of relief, thinking she had gone too far.

"I believe I am," she replied honestly.

"Look over the papers I prepared for you. I think you'll be extremely happy with what my company and I can do for you," London said. He reached over and took her hand in his, giving it a squeeze.

"I think I will." Khalil's gaze rested on London. Alana sat back and remained quiet. This was a pivotal moment. Was Khalil going to sign with London? "And you would be handling me?"

"Absolutely," London replied smoothly.

The waiter, Tom, returned to their table and began clearing the dishes. "I hope everyone enjoyed themselves. Anyone up for dessert?"

"Oh, I couldn't," Alana gushed, patting her belly. Khalil and London declined as well.

"Then I'll be back around with the check."

It had been fun watching London interact with Khalil and see him at work. At first, she'd had reservations about coming to dinner with them, but it turned out to be fine.

"The night is young. Why don't we head out and have some fun?" Khalil suggested.

Tom returned with the check. London pulled out his wallet and slid his credit card into the black leather receipt folder without even looking at the total.

"Where do you have in mind? Alana deserves a night out," London insisted, giving her a wink.

"Oh, um… sure. Whatever you guys want to do."

She didn't want to be a Debbie Downer on an important night for London. If Khalil signed with him, it would net London millions of dollars.

She bit back a sigh and stood from her chair, London immediately rising at her side. The waiter had returned, and London finished taking care of the check.

Khalil gave them a wide smile. "I have just the place in mind."

They made their way out of the restaurant where a few people unashamedly stopped Khalil, requesting selfies and autographs.

Before long, they were in London's luxury vehicle, driving through the city toward the Flats. Alana knew they were heading to one of the most popular clubs in the city.

London and Khalil were deep in conversation about what London could offer him. Apparently, Khalil had read the files that were sent over days ago.

London pulled up to the valet in front of a fancy nightclub.

This was not her scene.

She was never one to hang out at places like

this. Not that there was anything wrong with it. Clubbing just wasn't her thing.

She would try to have fun. This was what London did for a living, and if his client wanted to go to a club for a few drinks and music, then so be it.

Alana was out of her comfort zone. There were just too many people, the music was loud and crude.

They were in the VIP section of the club, seated in a half circle booth. From where Alana was, she could see the entire club. With her wineglass in hand, she remained quiet at her seat in the booth. London and Khalil were standing nearby, talking with a few other extremely tall men. They had to be athletes.

The champagne was flowing.

Alana just about had a heart attack when she saw the prices on the menu. This was London's world when he was courting athletes. Money apparently wasn't an issue when it came to catering to the millionaire athletes.

The group of men stood around, their laughter drawing the attention of the clubgoers.

Especially the women.

Alana was appalled by some of their outfits. The brazen women weren't the least bit shy when they approached Khalil.

She glanced over at London. The London she used to peek at through her peephole was present.

The charmer.

The businessman.

He knocked back a shot and sat his glass down on the table. Catching her eye, he motioned for her to come to him.

She shook her head at first. The music was so loud, she couldn't hear a thing of what anyone had to say.

He motioned to her again, his sexy grin in place.

She couldn't deny this man anything.

Standing, she made her way over to him.

"Fellas, I need to introduce you to my lady," London announced, wrapping an arm around her waist.

Alana blinked.

Did he just say she was his woman?

The newcomers nodded to her. They looked familiar, but she couldn't place from where.

Clutching her glass, she smiled nervously at them all.

"This is Liam, Mark, and Scott. They're all signed to Primetime," he informed her.

"Now I know why we haven't seen much of London." Liam laughed, reaching out to shake her hand.

"Is that a good thing or a bad thing?" she asked.

"Good thing," Mark chimed in, taking her hand next. "Are you signed to Primetime? I swear this man never quits working. The only thing that would stop him would be if he'd met a beautiful woman like you."

"No. We live in the same building."

"Don't worry about where I found her," London snorted. "And no, she doesn't have a sister."

They all shared a laugh. Alana scanned the area and found a bathroom located not too far from them.

"I'll be right back." In his ear, she whispered, "Bathroom."

"Hurry back."

Pressing a kiss to her cheek, she smiled and made her way to the ladies' room.

When she entered, she found a small line. Keeping to herself, she waited her turn as she listened to the women speak about the men they had their eyes on.

This was so not her.

Compared to their barely there dresses, Alana had played it safe with one that was formfitting, but allowed her to show off her curves, look feminine, and had brought a gleam of heat to London's eyes.

She wished Sofie was here with her, giving her a buffer. Alana and Sofie were notorious for people watching, and they would've had a ball tonight.

Her turn came up, and she quickly did her business. Washing her hands, she walked out and made her way toward London. A raucous cheer went up from where they were standing, and a waiter was delivering another round of shots. She hoped it meant that Khalil was signing with Primetime. London had worked so hard to woo the basketball star.

The bottom of Alana's stomach gave way at the sight of the women surrounding London and the guys. She took a deep breath and blew it out slowly, trying not to be the jealous woman. She knew who he was going home with, but it didn't mean she wouldn't scratch out the eyes of the ones standing too close to him. Khalil and the others, she couldn't care less about.

"Excuse me," she murmured, trying to make her way back to London. The women were crowding around, all trying to catch them an athlete, and apparently a sports agent.

Not on her watch, they weren't. They could have any of the athletes, but not her man.

She elbowed her way through until she stood next to a woman who was clearly trying to put the moves on London.

"I said, can we get out of here?" the blonde bimbo giggled.

"You sure can," Alana snapped, grabbing her attention. "But not with him."

"Excuse me?"

"Move."

Blondie's girlfriends pulled her away, apparently sensing the daggers Alana was shooting from her eyes.

London's eyes crinkled in the corners as he pulled her close to kiss her. Holding up her hand to block him, she looked closely to see how drunk he was.

"How drunk are you?" she asked.

"Not so drunk that I didn't realize that wasn't you." He pulled her close, a smile on his lips. "I didn't even know what she was saying. I swear."

"Is that so?"

After a moment of giving him a stern look, she leaned into him. His hand slid around to the swell of her ass and held her in place.

"When we leave here, I promise I'll prove it to you." He nuzzled her neck, and she melted against him.

*L*ondon found Alana had made it to the booth and took a seat. She looked out of sorts. He knew she wasn't a nightclub type of person.

Khalil and the fellas were just ramping up, with no signs of slowing down.

He couldn't torture her by keeping her out any later.

He motioned over to the waiter so he could settle the bill. Whenever he took clients out, he always footed the bill. It was a business transaction, and he'd send the receipts to his secretary on Monday morning.

"It's time for me to head home," he announced.

This was new for him. When courting a client, he would normally stay until the club closed. But one look at Alana, he knew he had to get them home.

"Take Alana home, man." Khalil gave him the one-armed hug. "She's something special."

"Don't I know it."

Alana had won Khalil over with her analytical advice.

He waved to Liam, Mark, and Scott. They were his clients, and he was sure they would talk about him when he left.

Which would be a good thing.

He had a great relationship with the three of them, and he was sure they would talk Khalil into signing with him.

Walking over to the booth, he held his hand out to Alana. "Come on, babe. Let's get you home."

"Are you sure? We don't have to leave if you're not ready," she protested.

With a nod, he assisted her up and out of the booth.

"Sir, the check." The waiter handed him a small

black portfolio that hid the receipt. London signed the small piece of paper, barely glancing at the total. What he spent tonight was nothing compared to what he stood to make off of Khalil signing with him.

"Can you bring over another bottle of Ace of Spades for my clients?" London asked, handing him back the signed receipt. It was Khalil's favorite, and London wanted his future client to be happy.

"Of course." The waiter took the crisp hundred-dollar bills London handed him. "I shall have your car brought around."

"Thanks."

Pulling Alana close to his side, he guided her through the thick crowd and headed toward the exit. Whenever the athletes partied, the amount of people who came to the clubs increased. Everyone wanted a chance to be in the same building as the stars. Having someone like Khalil in Cleveland would be good for the economy. Fans would flock to the city to watch him play basketball, which would mean more patrons to the downtown bars, restaurants, and clubs.

They arrived outside and waited for his car to be brought around.

"It won't look bad with you leaving now, will it?" Alana asked.

"Not at all." He dropped a kiss on her forehead. "Matter of fact, Khalil suggested I take you home."

Her eyes grew wide. "Was I that obvious?"

"Babe, I know this isn't you." He laughed, squeezing her tight. "I appreciate that you came with me."

"I don't know how you do it." She looked down the line of people waiting to get into the club. "It's late for me. I'm usually in my jammies, curled up on the couch, fighting sleep."

"At least you wouldn't be alone. You've got me."

"Are you okay to drive?" she asked as the car drove up the street.

"Yeah. My last few drinks were actually water."

London would have normally stayed and joined in on the drinking and partying, but he honestly preferred to spend his time with Alana.

An idea came to mind.

"Have any plans this weekend?"

"I don't."

The valet parked in front of them. A young man hopped out of the luxury vehicle and jogged around it to open the door for Alana.

"You do now."

Ushering her into the car, he shut the door and tipped the valet—a handsome tip—and got behind the wheel.

"Really?"

Grinning over at her, he buckled his seat belt and flipped on the turn signal, merging slowly into traffic.

"There's somewhere I want to take you."

He pressed down on the gas, expertly maneuvering his way through traffic toward the freeway.

"For the entire weekend?"

"Yup. Sit tight, darling. We'll be there soon."

"But I don't have clothes—"

He snorted. "Like you'll need them."

"Wait, what?" Her giggles filled the interior of the car.

"You'll see. I promise, you're going to love it."

Twenty minutes later, London drove the car down a winding driveway, lined with thick trees for privacy from the neighborhood. He'd found and purchased this gem two years ago. The first time he saw it, he had fallen in love with it.

"Alana, babe. We're here." He reached over and rubbed her thigh, interrupting her cute little snoring.

"Where are we?"

The sound of her husky voice sent a shot of desire to his cock. Tightening his grip on the steering wheel, he drove up to a waterfront mansion.

"This is my home."

"Home? But you have the condo. Why do you need both?" she inquired, pushing her thick hair behind her ear.

Killing the engine, he sat back in his seat and stared at the beautiful structure.

"When I moved to Cleveland, I wanted a home where I could entertain and live." The mansion had seven bedrooms and ten bathrooms. It was just too large for a single guy. Jaxon blew into town once in a while and would crash here, but it wasn't the same. "I got too lonely here."

"So why didn't you sell it?"

"Because I really do love it, and I figured it would be best for a family, not a business." Picking up her hand, he brought it to his lips and kissed the back of it. "Let me give you the tour."

Stepping out of the vehicle, he strolled over to her side and helped her out, keeping hold of her hand.

"I can't wait to see it during the daytime," Alana gushed.

"It's magnificent."

They walked along the short stone path that led to the large mahogany doors. They were unique and handcrafted with designs that were found throughout the entire house.

Unlocking the door, he stepped inside. He turned to find Alana still standing outside with her wide eyes locked on him.

"What is it?" he asked nervously.

"London, you are just filled with surprises."

Alana stepped over the threshold and gasped. Biting back a laugh, he shut the door behind her, locked it, then turned to watch her.

He wanted to see her reaction. For some strange reason, he wanted her to love this house as much as he did.

He needed her approval of it.

Alana took a few steps forward and spun around in a circle, shock lining her face as she took it all in. The foyer was a bit much. A winding cherry wood staircase was located next to the office. Pristine white marble floors were outlined by the wood. It was a unique contrast that worked.

A large glass table in the center of the room held a large vase filled with fresh flowers. A crystal chandelier hung overhead from the vaulted ceiling.

"London, this is beautiful," Alana raved, her face lit up in awe.

"That was the exact reaction I had when I first walked in here." Pushing away from the door, he walked over and gathered her into his arms. "Let me give you a tour."

Alana laid in the circle of London's arms.

She was impressed by the home. She didn't think she would like something that wasn't downtown and trendy, but this place had her picturing a family.

She sighed, unsure of when she began picturing little London's and little Alana's. Their children would be beautiful and smart, she was sure.

Their tour of the house was cut short. One kiss turned into three. A little tongue action, and London had her pressed up against the wall, pouring into her.

He had carried her into the bedroom after, and they'd been there ever since.

She stared out at the open sky from the large windows London had left open. The entire wall was made of glass, giving them a front-row seat to the magnificent nighttime backdrop filled with stars. Even the ceiling had skylights, giving glimpses of the sky.

She was sure the room would be filled with lots of natural light during the day.

"What are you thinking about?" London's deep voice inquired. She smiled, skimming her fingers along his abdomen.

"How suburb life might be better than downtown life."

"You like it here?"

Stroking the small of her back, a shiver rippled through her body.

"I just might with a little more persuasion," she proclaimed, grinning at him.

"Is that so?"

He guided her head to his, kissing her softly. Alana lost herself in the kiss. His tongue gently stroked hers, drawing hers into a slow dance.

Rolling her onto her back, her legs immediately parted, allowing him to settle into the valley of her thighs.

She gasped as the blunt tip of his cock nudged her entrance before he surged forward, sinking fully into her.

"London," she moaned. He trailed passionate

kisses along her jawline and nuzzled his face into the crook of her neck.

He withdrew slightly before thrusting harder.

"I was thinking…" He paused, shifting up onto his knees. Pressing his hands on the back of her thighs, he opened her wider. She dug her nails into the bedding, feeling more exposed and at his mercy. His hips rocked, sending him deeper inside. "We should stay here all weekend. Just the two of us."

Alana's eyes fluttered closed as she basked in the sensation of him fucking her. His movements grew bolder, harder, faster.

London was commanding her body, and she was willingly giving herself to him.

He wanted to lock them away in a million-dollar mansion for the weekend? So be it.

"**M**r. Keith, there's a Mr. Berry Jenkins on line one for you," his secretary announced. London looked at his desk phone, his heart leaping in his chest.

"Give me a second. I'll get it," London replied to Carol.

Berry Jenkins was Khalil's business manager.

It was Monday morning, and he was back in the office. As much as he loved working and making money, he had not been ready to come back to reality. The weekend at his suburban home had been magical. Alana was as in love with the home as he was.

They had spent the entire weekend blessing every room. He should've been tired from his sex filled days with Alana, but he wasn't.

Hell, he was growing stiff just thinking about her. He'd lost count of how many times they had made love.

Inviting her to his home had meant a lot to him. That was a place he'd never taken a woman to, but he hadn't shared that with her. It was a sensitive subject between them.

He'd had food delivered to them, and had refused to allow either of them to dress. That had made things very interesting.

Breathing deep, he picked up the phone. "This is London Keith."

"Mr. Keith, it's Berry Jenkins. How are you?"

"I'm doing well. I'm hoping you're calling with good news," London coaxed, cutting to the chase. He needed to know.

Was he going to be representing Khalil or not?

London had a good feeling that Khalil was won over by Alana alone. She had captivated the basketball star, giving him much to think about.

"You're straight forward, and that's something Khalil and I like about you."

"What's the point of beating around the bush? I'm always going to be honest with you."

"You can stop trying to sell us," Berry chuckled. London's breath caught in his throat. "You've sold us. Khalil with be signing with you."

London pumped his fist in the air. This was just what he needed.

"I'm so glad to hear that, Berry. Just know that I'll be working very hard for Khalil and the family."

Working with the athletes involved working with their families. London knew these contracts and endorsements were not only for the stars, but their families as well, and everyone they supported.

"I'm sure you are. We've heard a lot of good things about your company, and we're sure this will be a good fit."

"I'm sure of it. I'll have my secretary set up a meeting for the contract signing."

"You do that. Thursday is a good day for us."

"I can make that work."

After a few more details, he disconnected the call and jumped out of his seat, clapping and hollering with excitement.

This was exactly what he and Primetime needed. His reputation was paying off. He took care of his clients. The best thing for his business was word of mouth. No matter how hard he sold what his company could do, nothing was better than athletes talking amongst their peers and recommending him.

He needed to call Alana and share the news with her.

Snatching his phone from his desk, he placed a call to her. That morning, they had woken up bright and early to drive back to their apartment building where he'd left Alana, pouting. Apparently, she hadn't wanted to return to work, either.

She answered on the first ring.

"Hey, London."

Her soft, husky voice caused his cock to jerk.

"Hey, baby. Guess what?" He could barely contain his excitement.

"What is it?"

"Khalil's committing to Primetime."

"Oh my goodness! That's awesome. Congratulations. So what happens next?"

"The signing of the contracts will probably be Thursday, and I would love for you to be by my side."

He looked out the large window behind his desk. From where he stood, he could see Lake Erie.

"This Thursday? I won't be able to attend."

London blinked. This was monumental, and he wanted her there with him. She had a part in signing Khalil whether she knew it or not.

"Why not?"

"I just found out I need to fly to Chicago tomorrow, but I'll be home on Friday. You and I can celebrate when I get back."

"Do you really need to go? Can't they send someone else?"

"It doesn't work like, London. I'm not the owner or manager. They say I have to go, then I go."

He ran a hand along his face. This was a big deal, and he needed her with him. There had to be something she could do.

"But why you? Isn't there someone else who's just as qualified to go to take your place?"

"London, I'm proud of you, honey, but I have to work. I don't bring in millions of dollars. I have bills to pay, and if I want to continue to pay them, then I'll be going to Chicago." Her voice grew curt. He knew he was pushing her, but he wanted her there.

"Bills? If you need—"

"Don't you dare, London Keith," she snapped, cutting him off. "I can take care of myself. I just need you to realize that my job is important."

He needed to shut up before he really put his foot in his mouth.

"Alana, I know that, and I'm sorry. I was just caught up in the excitement and really wanted you there."

Her voice softened. "I know. And I promise when I come home, we'll have our own private celebration."

"Mr. Keith, your brother is on line two," Carol announced through the intercom.

"I've got to go, babe. That's Jaxon calling."

"I'll talk to you later."

They disconnected their call, and he couldn't help but stare at the phone for a second more before walking back to his desk.

"Yo, little brother."

"Tell me you've got good news. I'm hearing through the grapevine that you may have snagged Khalil."

"Little brother, one day you're going to realize how much of a genius I am." London grinned. "We have a celebration to plan. Khalil will be signing this week."

"Hot damn! Then I'm flying into town. I'm proud of you, big bro. This is going to be all the talk."

"Hurry up and get here. We need to strategize media, the celebration, and getting all negotiations on the table. We're going down in history."

"Oh, God. Bed, you look so inviting," Alana groaned, walking out of the hotel bathroom wrapped in a towel. She was drained and couldn't wait to go back home. The trip to Chicago was a nightmare. The office here was in complete disarray, and she and her team were sent to bring the Chicago office up-to-date with theirs.

One day, and she was ready to pull her hair out. But at least they had made great headway. She was able to get their team up to speed on a lot of the processes that she had developed to help spearhead her department. She had developed some modeling techniques that had saved the company a ton of money, and her manager wanted her to share them with the struggling office.

Flopping down onto the bed, she tucked her feet underneath her. She hated leaving Cleveland. London had really been pushing for her to stay so she could be with him during the signing and the celebration they were going to throw for Khalil choosing London's company to represent him.

But he'd wanted her to abandon her responsibilities to support him.

Her job was important to her. She was an independent woman who could take care of herself. She didn't know what type of women he was involved with before—

She stopped.

Yes, she did.

Floozies.

Whores.

Women who only wanted to fuck and take money from him.

She cringed. Hopefully not in that order. London Keith didn't need to hire prostitutes. The women were practically tripping over themselves to get into his apartment before she came along.

All he wanted was to celebrate the biggest contract of his career.

God. Now she felt horrible.

Her work was practically done here. She had

given them manuals and helped install the work-sheets for all the analysts. Anything else they could do via Zoom.

Alana grinned. She would cut her trip short and surprise London.

Grabbing her phone from the nightstand, she dialed London's number.

The phone rang, and soon his voicemail picked up. She opted out of leaving a message. He would be crazy busy at the moment.

She opened up Instagram, and the first post she saw was of Primetime Sports Management. It was a video posted earlier that day with the official press release announcement that Khalil was going to be represented by Primetime. She watched London and Khalil answer questions, and Khalil speak for few minutes.

Alana was proud of London. All of his hard work was paying off.

She scrolled to the next post.

Her stomach clenched at the photos of Khalil, London, and a few other men she didn't know posing for the camera. The snapshot itself didn't bother her. It was the strippers behind the group.

She understood the business of courting athletes, but seeing London hanging with the men in that type of establishment didn't sit right with her.

Should the company be posting pictures of celebrities in strip clubs?

Was that appropriate publicity?

She scrolled a little more and saw videos of them drinking, tossing an obscene amount of money at the strippers dancing around for them. Her heart raced.

This was the old London. The one she would stalk from behind her apartment door. She cringed at the photos of women hanging around him.

She scrolled and landed on Khalil's page. There were videos of the strippers grinding and dancing in front of him and London.

Alana closed the app, refusing to get caught up in things she saw on social media. There hadn't been any reason why she couldn't trust London, and she wasn't going to start making assumptions now.

"He's celebrating with his new client. Everything is fine." Putting on her jammies, she climbed back into bed. She'd look in the morning for an afternoon flight home, and would be able to join him in celebrating.

lana walked out of her bedroom, wearing a cute little dress she had picked up from a boutique that was located in the lobby of her hotel. Going into the kitchen, she opened her fridge and pulled out a bottle of wine she'd stashed away before she had left.

"After the week I had, this is well-deserved." She spun around and took out a glass from her cabinet and poured a healthy amount.

Glancing at her watch, she grinned. London should be home at any moment, and she couldn't wait to see the look on his face.

It would be pointless to even put on shoes, knowing her man would be taking the dress off and dropping it on the floor.

Setting the almost empty bottle onto the counter, she ambled into the living room.

Earlier that morning, she had texted him, but didn't want to ruin the surprise. He'd mentioned some gathering at their office. Hopefully, he wouldn't be too much longer.

Sipping her wine, she turned on the television and flipped the channel to ESPN. The hosts of the show were speaking of Khalil and the new sports agency he'd signed with.

"Primetime is becoming a powerhouse. Who isn't signing with them?" a black man in a navy suit asked. He was handsome. If she remembered right, he was a former basketball player.

"London and Jaxon Keith are geniuses when it comes to contract negotiations. They've built their empire from scratch. There isn't anything these brothers won't do for their clients," the other anchor commented.

London had shared with her that his younger brother would be in town to celebrate, and she couldn't wait to meet him.

She watched as they continued to talk about the

upcoming contract negotiations of the NBA. Trade deals, and the amount of money they were discussing was staggering.

"I think I made the wrong decision in life," she murmured. "I should've been a basketball star."

A giggle escaped her. At her height, basketball would never have been in her future.

Muffled laughter could be heard out in the hall-way. Her heart skipped a beat at the thought of seeing London.

Finishing her drink, she sat the empty glass down on the coffee table and walked over to her door, excitement brimming throughout her body. Three days away from London was too long.

Standing on her tiptoes, she peeked out the hole and froze.

The floor of her stomach gave way. Nausea rose until she thought she was about to lose the wine she had drank.

London was leading two women into his apart-ment—one blonde, one brunette.

Pain rippled through her chest.

London was cheating on her?

She wasn't supposed to be back in town until tomorrow.

While he thought she was away, he was returning to his old self.

Alana inhaled sharply, trying to push the bile down. There had to be a better explanation.

She turned away from the door and stood still.

Should she go over there and bang on the door?

Did she really want to confront him while he was in the middle of doing God knew what with those skanks?

She made her way back to the couch and flopped down onto it.

No, she would wait.

She would approach this like an adult.

Settling back on the couch, she willed herself not to cry. She'd be damned if he would cause her to cry.

In the back of her mind, it all seemed too good to be true. London Keith dating someone like herself? They were complete opposites.

Those women who followed him into the apartment looked as if they had just strolled off the runway.

There was no way a short, chubby girl with glasses could compete with them.

She was lucky she had that first night that

turned into an entire weekend. She'd gotten more than she bargained for.

But did it have to hurt so damn bad? Her eyes grew blurry from unshed tears.

Dammit, she would not cry.

She swiped angrily at her eyes and breathed deeply, in and out. There was no use in crying.

Alana knew the type of man London was. He was who he was, and probably grew bored of the quiet life with her.

There was no changing a man. She knew better, and now felt stupid to think that he would want to be in an actual relationship with her.

She had basically given him what he wanted.

A good fuck buddy who lived across the hall.

Pushing off the couch, she walked into her bedroom and stripped off the dress. That was a wasted purchase.

Diving into the bed in only her undies, she snuggled under her blanket, feeling crushed and betrayed.

He'd introduced her to his clients as his lady.

Did that truly mean anything to him?

Or was that some term men threw out casually?

London dialed Alana's number for the fifth time, all his calls going to voicemail. He wasn't sure what was going on. She should've been back from Chicago by now. She'd said Friday, so did something change?

Why wouldn't she have called him when she got home?

He leaned back on the chaise on the veranda of his mansion. It was a beautiful night, and he was waiting for her to call to let him know when she was back in Cleveland.

He wanted to scoop her up and bring her to his home.

After the week he'd had, he just wanted to relax and enjoy some peace and quiet.

Resting his phone on his lap, he reached for his glass of bourbon and took a sip as he stared off at the landscape. Time spent out here would be perfect if Alana were here.

He took another sip of his drink, the amber liquid burning on its way down.

"Where are you, Alana?" he murmured.

Picking up his phone, he stared at it.

Something wasn't sitting right with him.

Getting to his feet, he made his way through the house. He was going to her apartment.

Minutes later, he was driving along the winding road that led to the highway. He wasn't much of a praying man, but he sent up a small request, asking for her to be okay.

She was probably already in the bed.

He grinned, imagining crawling in next to her. He'd teach her about returning to town and not calling.

He drove into the underground parking lot and pulled into his spot. Exiting the vehicle, he headed toward the elevator, tossing his keys up in the air and catching them.

The few days away from Alana got him to thinking. He wanted more from what they had. Stopping in front of the elevator, he hit the button.

He never would have thought he'd be thinking of asking a woman to move in with him, but Alana was perfect for him.

She kept him grounded.

When the doors opened to the elevator, he got inside and hit the button for their floor.

He was sure he was grinning like an idiot.

Yeah, he'd ask her to move in with him. As much as she loved the mansion, they could move in there. He'd keep the condo for when Jaxon came to town, and she could sell hers.

It would be perfect.

He arrived at their floor and strolled down the hall toward their apartments. He glanced down at his watch. Yes, she should have been home by now. She hadn't wanted him to pick her up.

Stopping in front of Alana's door, he paused, feeling the butterflies fluttering around in his stomach.

He couldn't remember the last time he was ever this nervous.

He rapped on her door.

The faint sound of her television could be heard coming from inside. A few moments later, the door opened partially.

Alana peered through the opening. She was dressed in shorts, a tank, and had her leopard print bonnet on her head. She stared at him through large black glasses.

"Babe. When were you going to call and tell me you made it back safe?" he asked.

Alarms went off in the back of his head.

One look at her face told him something was wrong.

She didn't open the door fully, and appeared guarded.

"Khalil agreed to sign on with my agency.

Remember?" he said, trying to ignore the voices. He smiled, but she didn't return it.

"I remember." Leaning against the doorjamb, she stared at him. "You must have had a wild night celebrating."

He frowned, running a hand through his hair. "Not really."

He reached for her hand to pull her to him, but she moved away.

What the hell was wrong?

He racked his brain, trying to think of what he could've done.

"Baby, what's wrong?" He reached for her again, but she backed away.

"Don't call me that," she sniffed.

"Alana, what are you talking about? What did I do?"

"What did you do?" His heart ached at the sight of her tears sliding down her cheeks. "Do you think I'm stupid? Go call whoever you were with last night, *baby*."

"Last night? I stayed at my house last night."

"Oh, I know. Just stay over in your place, and never knock on my door again."

With that, she slammed the door shut.

London stood there, stunned.

What the hell just happened?

Turning, he went over to his apartment, unlocked the door, and stepped inside.

He didn't know how he went from flying on top of the world to falling down to the depths of hell.

"I guess I didn't mean anything to him after all," Alana murmured, snuggling up under her blanket on the couch, trying to watch television.

The giggling and non-stop partying was pissing her off.

Nausea rolled through her.

Of course, while London was partying it up and living the good life, she came down with some nasty bug. It had been two weeks since she'd cut all ties with him.

But that didn't mean anything.

He was everywhere.

Television. Newspapers. Radio.

Everyone was talking about Khalil coming to Cleveland, thanks to London Keith. Not only was Cleveland gaining one of the best basketball players of all time, but London had negotiated the craziest deal any professional athlete had received.

She couldn't help but see him anywhere and everywhere she looked.

This was the same London who had broken her heart.

As much as she wanted to hate him, she was proud of him. He'd worked so hard to get his client, and he'd succeeded.

She tried to avoid anyplace she would see him. Her new routine was work, then home, until lately. She'd been cooped up in the condo for the last two days, feeling as though she were dying.

Reaching for her ginger ale, she took a sip before putting the can back on the coffee table. She tried to focus on the movie, but all she could hear was the thumping music coming from London's apartment.

It was as if he was purposely trying to piss her off.

There was a knock at the door.

"Finally," she groaned. Sofie had promised to stop over after work.

Using all her strength to push up off the couch, she stumbled over to the door, still wrapped in her blanket. Opening it, she found Sofie standing in the hallway with a wide smile on her lips.

"God, you look like shit," Sofie huffed, coming into the apartment carrying a few bags.

"I love you too," Alana mumbled, following her into the kitchen.

"I know you do." Laughing, she sat her bags down on the counter and turned back to Alana. "I brought enough drugs to wipe out whatever ails you."

"Good. I just want to go to sleep for days."

She hadn't been sleeping well at all. Each night she'd toss and turn, remembering the sight of London walking into his apartment with those sluts.

It had plagued her like a nightmare that wouldn't go away.

Why hadn't he just broken up with her?

She would've respected honesty. If he was done with her, he could've been man enough to admit he didn't want to be with her anymore. Instead, he'd acted as if he didn't know what she was talking about.

It was childish, and she really didn't expect that from him. Both of them were too old to play high school games.

"What are your symptoms?" Sofie asked, setting her purchases out on the counter.

"I'm stuffy, nauseated, and my body aches."

"Hmm… Here's some cold medicine," she offered, holding out a box.

Alana took the box and read the back of it.

"I brought soup, and even hot chocolate. Go get back on the couch and I'll heat the soup for you."

"You're the bestest friend a girl could ever have."

Her heart was broken, and all she needed was her best friend to come over and take care of her. How did she get to be so lucky? She didn't have her parents to lean on or any siblings. Sofie was the closest thing to family.

"Aw, Alana. I'm here." Sofie wrapped her in a tight hug. "Now go. I got this."

Making her way back to the couch, she inhaled sharply, trying to will the bile threatening to come up to go back down.

She tucked her feet underneath her and waited patiently for Sofie. Her friend wasn't much of a cook, so it was no surprise when she heard the microwave turn on.

Minutes later, she came into the living room, carrying her lap tray with a steaming bowl of soup and crackers.

"You are a godsend."

Taking the tray from Sofie, she picked up her spoon and dipped it into the soup. After blowing on it, she sipped the broth and sighed.

It was oh so good.

Sofie darted back into the kitchen before retiring with a healthy sized glass of wine.

"Now tell me what happened?" Sofie demanded, taking a seat on the edge of the couch. "Don't leave out any details."

She really didn't want to talk about it, but she knew she could trust her friend. Taking small spoonfuls of her soup, she shared the story of her and London's demise.

"And I thought he was going to be different, that he really liked me."

Alana stared down at her empty bowl. She hadn't thought she would eat it all at first, but it seemed her body needed it.

Sofie stood, having finished her third glass of wine.

Alana eyed her warily. When Sofie was tipsy, there was no telling what she'd say or do.

"The bastard," Sofie swore, resting her hands on her waist. "I say we march over to his apartment and confront him."

Alana's eyes grew wide. "What?"

She had said her piece and was done with him. She didn't want to see him. It had taken everything she had to avoid him.

"We're going over there. He's going to give me a piece of my mind."

"That doesn't even make sense," Alana groaned. Yup, her friend was tipsy.

Sofie spun around and stalked toward the front door.

Alana set her lap tray on the coffee table and got off the couch, taking off after Sofie.

"You're in no mind to go yell at someone."

"I'm not that drunk. I just need to yell at the man who made my best friend cry," she snapped. She was out the door and in the hallway in the blink of an eye.

"Sheesh," Alana whispered. Whatever sickness this was had her feeing under the weather. She made it out into the hallway, just in time for Sofie to bang on the door. Alana rolled her eyes. She was sure the neighbors around the corner had heard the ruckus. "What are you, the police?"

Sofie shrugged. "With the music blasting, he may not hear us."

The door swung open, startling them.

Alana turned to the door and froze in place.

Sofie stood froze next to her and turned her attention to Alana.

"Can I help you?" he asked.

That was not London.

He looked similar to London, but he wasn't. He was about the same height, slightly leaner, a light scar on his chin. He kept his hair a little longer than London did.

"Who are you?" Alana asked, her heart pounding in her chest. She already knew the answer. Her palms grew sweaty as she stared at him.

"Jaxon." He leaned against the doorjamb, grinning at Sofie, his Southern drawl just as thick as London's. "And you are?"

"I'm Sofie," she answered, annoyed. She rolled her eyes and motioned to Alana. "This is Alana."

"Where's London?" Alana asked, finally able to compose herself. She needed to speak with him, now.

"He's at home." Jaxon folded his arms over his

wide chest. He and London had similar features, but one could definitely tell the brothers apart. Alana's chest constricted.

Oh, God.

Had she made a mistake?

"As in, in there?" Alana pointed into London's condo. "Or at his house in the suburbs?"

"Not sure why, but he moved out of here two weeks ago, like the gates of hell had opened. The bastard wouldn't tell me why, either. He's been staying at the lakefront house ever since." Jaxon straightened to his full height, towering over both of them, his gaze going back to Sofie. "I'm having a small get-together, and you two are more than welcome to join us."

"Nah. We're good."

Grabbing Alana's arm, Sofie practically dragged her back into her apartment.

"Suit yourself. Change your mind, just come back over," Jaxon offered with a laugh.

Sofie slammed the door to Alana's apartment shut and barked, "What the hell is going on?"

Alana stood frozen in place, unsure.

"Oh, God. Did I confuse them?"

The bottom of her stomach gave way.

She rushed through her apartment and ran into

the guest bathroom. Falling to her knees in front of the toilet, she made it just in time for the contents of her stomach to make their reappearance.

"Are you okay?" Sofie asked from the doorway.

Alana wiped her mouth with the back of her hand.

No, she was far from okay.

She had mistaken Jaxon for London.

She had done something horrible. She'd assumed he'd went back to his old ways, and hadn't even given him a chance to explain.

"I made a mistake," she cried out, her vision blurred with tears.

"Here, let's get you cleaned up, and then you can call London." Sofie came into the small bathroom and helped her up off the floor.

"He probably won't speak with me," Alana sniffed.

"You won't know unless you try."

London walked into his bedroom, wrapping a towel around his waist. The hot shower had helped relax his weary muscles.

All he wanted to do was get in the bed and sleep.

He hadn't been able to rest much. All he could see when he closed his eyes was Alana, standing in her doorway with tears in her eyes.

He didn't know what he had done to cause her to break up with him. He had pored over everything he could think of.

He grimaced when he remembered the leaked

videos and photos on his company's social media pages. He'd had to reprimand the young guy who was in charge of Primetime's online accounts.

The videos and photos hadn't been professional.

That was the only thing he could think of that had possibly set Alana off.

But it wasn't horrible. So they'd gone to a strip club. It was unfortunately part of his job when dealing with rich celebrities.

London exhaled and sat on the edge of his bed. Picking up his phone, he saw he had a missed call from Alana.

Before he could hit her number, Jaxon's picture came across the screen. London hit the accept button.

Sighing, he answered the call with, "What is it?"

"Well, hello to you too, big brother," Jaxon chuckled.

"What do you want, Jax?"

Standing, he finished drying himself off and snagged a pair of basketball shorts off his bed. Throwing them on, he walked over and hung the towel on the hook.

"Have you met your neighbors?" Jax asked.

London frowned and walked out of his bedroom. His body was already starting to ache. He had completed a brutal workout, trying to tire himself out.

"Yeah, I have. Why?"

Jogging down the stairs, he headed toward the kitchen, trying not to think of the weekend he had brought Alana here, where he'd taken her in pretty much every room.

Entering the kitchen, his gaze landed on the large island.

Fuck.

The second day Alana had stayed over, he had spread her out on the island and had her for lunch.

He could still hear her scream as she orgasmed.

Shaking his head, he made his way to the fridge.

"So, I'm entertaining some exquisite ladies, and these two chicks come banging on the door. A short one with huge glasses, and a taller one shaped like a Greek goddess," Jaxon began.

London inhaled sharply.

Short with huge glasses.

That would be Alana.

His Alana.

What was she doing there?

"Okay?" London paused, waiting to see what else his brother had to say.

"I don't know what was wrong with the shorter one—"

"What do you mean?" London snapped.

"She looked like death warmed over," Jaxon replied. "Anyway, they both seemed to be confused when they saw me."

"What do you mean, she looked like death warmed over?" London stalked out of the kitchen, forgetting what he had gone in there for to begin with. If something was wrong with Alana, he had to go to her.

"As in, the woman was sick," Jaxon advised, exasperated.

"I've got to go. I'll call you back."

Hanging up on his brother, he found a clean T-shirt in the laundry room and threw on his tennis shoes. He was out the door in five minutes flat and speeding down the driveway.

A sense a déjà vu filled London as he marched down the hall toward Alana's apartment. This time, the door opened, and her friend Sofie stepped out into the hallway and shut the door. They'd met a few times, but he hadn't really spent time with her.

Sofie cleared her throat. "London."

"Where's Alana?" he demanded.

"She's inside. She's not feeling well."

"I need to see her."

Brushing past her, he banged on the door.

"I just got her into bed. Can't you wait——"

"No."

He didn't care that Alana was pissed at him. He would apologize, and they would talk about it. Right now, he had to see her with his own eyes to make sure she was okay.

"Alana!"

He knew he was causing a ruckus, but he could care less.

The door opened, and Alana stood there in her nightshirt that stopped mid-thigh, and her bonnet. Not having her glasses on, she squinted up at him.

Pushing the door open, he made his way into her apartment, his heart sinking. She looked miserable.

"What are you doing here?" she asked, taking a step back.

"I heard you were sick."

"I tried to tell him you weren't feeling well," Sofie huffed.

"It's okay, Sofie. I'm good." Alana smiled softly. "I'll call you tomorrow."

"Okay." Sofie hesitated, her gaze darting back and forth between them. With a wave, she left out the door, shutting it gently behind her.

"What's wrong, babe?" he asked as he stepped forward, wanting to hold her.

She held up a hand and grimaced. "You shouldn't come close. I could be contagious."

"I don't care." He pulled her to him and wrapped his arms around her. It felt so good to feel her soft form against him. "We need to talk, Alana."

"We do," she sniffed, her forehead lying against his chest. He slid a hand to her forehead, not sensing a fever.

"Let's get you to bed," Scooping her up into his arms, he carefully carried her back into her bedroom.

"If you get sick, I'm not responsible," she joked.

"I'll be fine."

Laying her down, he pulled the covers over her as she leaned back against the pillows, facing him. He took a seat on the edge of the bed, taking her in. Even though she was sick, she was still the most beautiful woman in the world.

"Who told you I was sick?" she asked.

"Jaxon called to say two weird women came over, and one looked like death warmed over," he chuckled.

She stiffened.

He wasn't sure why.

Reaching for her hand, he laced their fingers together.

"Look, I just want to explain some things," he began, studying their hands, taking in the darker contrast of her skin against his. "I'm sure you saw some things online, and I want to say that going out to clubs and parties comes with the job, unfortunately. Before, I would get caught up in everything and enjoy myself immensely."

"I remember."

Looking into her brown eyes, he pressed a kiss to the back of her hand.

"But then I met you, and everything changed. You're all I think about. It's you I want to be with."

He wasn't going to go much deeper than this for the moment. He could wait until she felt better to have the conversation about them moving in together.

"I saw your Instagram page, and I may have gotten a little upset," she admitted, her grip on his hand tightening. "I don't like seeing women hanging all over you and trying to get your attention. I know I don't look like them—"

"What?" He narrowed his gaze on her. What the hell was she talking about? She was gorgeous.

"Don't patronize me. I'm not tall or thin. I don't fit the type of women you usually dated."

"Do you honestly think you aren't beautiful?"

He still hated that she saw the parade of women who came and went when she looked at him.

"It's not about me thinking I'm beautiful. It's knowing that I probably won't be able to hold your attention for long. I'm different. How long until you're bored with the geeky girl next door?"

She released his hand and pushed up higher on the bed.

"Is that what you think? That I'm with you because you're some flavor of the month I'll soon tire of?" He was starting to get pissed.

She nibbled on her lip and stared at him, not saying a word.

He stood and stepped away, running a hand through his hair. He was frustrated. He had never given her any reason to think something like this.

Where was this coming from?

"Alana, I care for you. I love the time we've spent together. I—"

The words '*I love you*' were close to spilling from his lips.

Did he love Alana?

Yes.

Without a doubt.

She had quickly become his entire world, his thoughts always filled with her. He hadn't even looked at another woman since they'd started their relationship.

"I left Chicago a day early, wanting to surprise you," she said softly.

He jerked around and looked at her staring down her hands.

"What?"

"I wanted to surprise you. I got so jealous over the women at the clubs, so I figured I would come home and celebrate with you. But then I heard giggling in the hallway, and when I went to the door, I saw you go into the apartment with a couple of girls."

"Me? After the club, I went to my house. Jaxon—"

He stopped and stared at her.

Fuck me sideways.

Jaxon had stayed at the apartment.

"I thought he was you."

He took a step back, feeling as though he'd taken a blow to the gut. Swallowing hard, he rubbed his chin.

"So you thought I would fuck other women while you were supposed to be out of town?" He couldn't believe it. Resting his hands on his waist, he stared up at the ceiling. "You really think I'm that type of guy?"

"You said you had a younger brother. You didn't say you were twins!" she cried out.

He and Jaxon were twins. He was older than his brother by a few minutes, and he always called Jaxon his younger brother, because he was. They were genetically identical, but there were noticeable differences between them.

"Even if I never mentioned we were twins, you didn't think to bring this up when I was here two weeks ago? That's what that was about? You thought I'd cheated on you?"

Biting her lip, she nodded. Big fat tears spilled from her eyes and rolled down her cheeks.

"You didn't ask. You didn't want to confront me to find out the truth. You didn't even want to fight for what we had. You just shut me out."

"I know what I saw," she hiccupped.

"That was my brother!" London hollered.

He inhaled sharply, not wanting to lose his temper. He was trying to remember she was ill.

This wasn't the time for them to talk, so he backed away.

"I want you to know that I would never have cheated on you. I care about you, deeply. No one means more to me than you. But if you can't trust me, then we might as well stop while we're ahead."

Spinning on his heel, he stormed out of the bedroom.

Pain filled his heart at the sound of her crying as he left the apartment and shut the door behind him. He stood in the hallway and stared at his apartment door, his chest rising and falling fast.

Music could be heard coming from inside. There was no way he could go in there. No doubt his brother still had guests over.

Blowing out a deep breath, London made the long, lonely trip back to his suburban home.

He thought he and Alana could have a future, but it looked as if his past reared its ugly head and bit him in the ass.

"I am so stupid," Alana sniffed, staring down at the coffee cupped between her hands.

"You are not. There has to be blame on both sides here. Why didn't he tell you they were identical twins?" Sofie asked. Reaching across the table, she rested her hand on Alana's knee. "That's a big deal. I'm sure he's used to being confused with his brother. I mean, they look just alike."

Once she got a good look at Jaxon, she could tell the difference. They were identical, but the look in his eyes was different. He had a small cut above his lip, and his hair wasn't styled the way London always did it.

Alana offered Sophie a small smile; it was all she could muster. Sighing, she took in the crowd at 216 Beans, with its steady flow of patrons coming and going. A few regulars were posted at their usual tables, working on their computers, tablets, or just going through their phones.

This had been her sanctuary away from home, but now she could only think about the first time she had brought London here.

"He was right. I didn't trust him." She took a sip of her drink and shivered. Two weeks had gone by since London had walked out of her condo. Every day since, their last conversation played over and over in her head.

What happened?

But she knew. It was because of her insecurities.

They were from two different worlds, and she just didn't want to believe that he would really want to be with someone like her.

"Well, I hate to say that you two didn't have the best communications," Sofie snorted. She shook her head and drank her coffee. Her brown eyes narrowed on Alana.

"What are you talking about?"

"You two were too busy playing 'sink the wiener' to really converse."

"What?" Alana giggled. Her friend had officially lost her marbles. "Sink the wiener? Who talks like that?"

"I don't know." Sofie laughed. "It was the first thing that came to my head."

This was why she needed her best friend. Without Sofie at a time like this, she would be curled up in bed in three-day-old pajamas, no shower, and eating ice cream while watching reruns of her favorite television shows.

"So what are you going to do?" Sofie asked softly.

Alana shrugged. She wasn't ashamed to admit that she missed London fiercely. In their short time together, they had grown close. Not only as lovers, but as friends.

They were the total package.

"I hurt him—bad." Finishing her coffee, Alana sat the empty cup down and took in the pedestrians walking past the window.

What did she want to do?

She wanted to get her man back. She wished she could go back in time and changed her reactions.

She should have gone over and pounded on his door, demanding to know what the hell was going on. Had she done that, they could have avoided all of this.

"But you're hurting too. Like I said, you're both at fault for your parts in this." Sofie's concerned eyes met hers. "Has he even reached out to you?"

Alana shook her head. She didn't blame him at all. What she had done was horrible. She wouldn't even speak to her if the roles were reversed.

She had blocked his business and personal pages on social media. She had heard people say that social media was the devil, and they weren't lying.

"We had something good. We could be ourselves with each other. I really got to know London Keith, not Mr. Hotness. He's a great guy, and I really miss him."

"I'm going to ask you again: What are you going to do? Leave him alone and move on with your life, or go after your man?" Sofie asked.

Alana couldn't imagine moving on. She didn't want to be with any other man. Hell, she grew angry inside just thinking of some other woman taking her place.

She pounded her fist on the table and declared, "I'm going after my man!"

No more would she mourn the loss of their relationship. She was going to fix this. London was hers, and she was going to fight for him.

"Damn straight you are." Grinning, Sophie mimicked Alana's action and pounded her fist on the table. "And how are you going to do that?"

Alana froze.

How would she go about getting London back?

Briefly, she thought of driving out to his home in the suburbs and banging on the door, demanding he take her back, but she knew that wouldn't work.

Sofie was right. Most of their relationship had been spent having lots of sex. Hell, with a man who looked like him, and was good at giving her orgasms, could anyone blame her?

She thought back to the times they shared things with each other. There were some nights—after a raunchy round of sex—they would stay up all night, talking about their childhood to their college years, and fun things they liked to do.

But one thing stood out to her.

Their first non-date.

A plan formed in her head.

"I know what it is I should do." She pushed her

glasses up the bridge of her nose and grabbed her purse.

Sofie's eyes lit up with excitement. "What?"

"Come on." Quickly clearing off their table, they exited the coffee shop, and Alana led the way down the street.

"Where are we going?" Sofie laughed, trying to keep up with her.

A few minutes later, they arrived at her favorite book store.

With Sofie hot on her heels, Alana made a beeline for the records section of the store, her heart racing. One thing London had said was that he missed old-school music. She thought of the expression on his face when he spoke of how he and his parents enjoyed listening to it together.

She would give him that. If he never wanted to talk to her again, she would make sure he had one thing that would comfort him with thoughts of home.

Music.

"Old records?" Sofie questioned, scratching her head. "I'm lost."

"He's in to old-school music. It has to do with his childhood." Alana began browsing through the records, not sure of what all to get, but she was certain of one album she had to find. She just prayed it hadn't been sold yet.

"Oh, is that what you're going to do to that man? Break him down to where he has no choice but to take you back?" Eyes alight, Sofie started going through the albums in front of her. "I like your style, sis."

Alana grinned, feeling excited for the first time in a while. This had to work.

Another plan popped up into her head.

She froze for a moment and knew it would be something she needed to do, but she wasn't too sure if she could pull it off.

Returning home, Alana placed her bags down on the couch. Because Sofie had picked up the evening shift at the hospital, she'd ditched her to get ready for work.

Having found the perfect gifts to send to London, Alana had gone to the post office and overnighted the package to London.

This was going to be a test.

Would she win him back?

Her anxiety level was through the roof. She had

never pursued a man before, let alone try to make up with one. When she broke up with Danny, she was relieved, and didn't look back. Well, except to use him as a reminder of what she didn't want in a man.

She prayed it would work. If not, she wouldn't be above begging for a second chance. She just hoped she wasn't too late, because women flocked to London—

Nope. She wasn't going to go down that trail of thinking.

London wasn't like that. He wouldn't do her that way. She saw the look in his eyes before he turned away from her and he had been crushed.

She had done that to him. Because of her insecurities, she ruined a good thing between them. That man had gone above and beyond, trying to show her how much he cared for her, how much he wanted her, and how sexy she was to him.

He wanted her just the way she was.

A short, chubby, nerdy girl next door.

A sudden wave a nausea came over her.

What the hell was that?

She stood there by the couch, trying to decide if she should make a run for the bathroom. Taking a few deep breaths, the sour feeling passed.

Swallowing hard, she stared at the door, knowing what she had to do if this plan of hers was going to work.

Alana marched out of her condo, crossed the hall, and knocked on his door. Her pulse raced at this crazy plan, but it was something that had to be done.

Footsteps sounded from behind the door, and within seconds, London's exact replica appeared in front of her. She immediately noted the differences between London and his brother. Her pulse began to calm, and she could breathe easier.

"Hello." She pushed her glasses up the bridge of her nose. "Jaxon, right?"

"Yeah." He folded his arms and leaned against the doorframe. "You're the chick from across the hall, right?"

"I am. My name is Alana. Alana Thornton." She held out her hand, and he gave it a firm shake.

"So you're the one who finally snagged my brother?"

"Snagged? Well, if starting a relationship with him, then ruining it by assuming the worst, making a mess of things and driving him away means I snagged him..." Pausing, she took a deep breath. It was either ramble on or cry. "Then yeah, that's me."

Jaxon stared at her without saying a word. She couldn't read him at all, and it was causing the hair on the back of her neck to stand up. This was probably a huge mistake.

"He's not here. You know he moved out and is staying at the house."

"I know. I'm here to ask a favor of you." His eyebrows shot up, and at that moment, he truly looked identical to London, making her sad. She needed to get London back.

"A favor of me?"

Pulling her phone out of her back pocket, she held it at the ready, willing her hand not to shake, and blurted out, "Can I have your mother's phone number?"

Raising his brow, he rattled off the number while Alana programmed it in and slowly backed away.

"Thanks." Turning, she walked over to her door, but paused and turned back to him. "Can we keep this between us?"

Jaxon's lips spread into a wide grin that looked so much like London's.

"I ain't saying nothing to that stubborn big

brother of mine. I want to see how this plays out."

Smiling, she relaxed. If she ever got to know Jaxon, she was sure they would get along just fine.

"Thanks." She gave him a wave and headed back inside her condo. Closing the door, she leaned back against it and breathed a sigh of relief. That was done, and now came the hard part.

Taking a seat on the couch, she called the number before she could chicken out. Leaning back in her seat, she kicked off her shoes and tucked her feet underneath her.

"Hello?" a feminine southern voice answered.

"May I speak with Mrs. Keith, please?"

"This is she. May I ask who's calling?"

Alana inhaled and closed her eyes. She hadn't spoken with this woman before, and wasn't even sure London had told his parents about her.

"Yes, ma'am. My name is Alana Thornton. I'm London's girlfriend." She paused as the pain in her heart spread. "Well, I *was* his girlfriend. I messed up, and I wanted to reach out to you for your help in winning him back."

The line drew silent.

Alana glanced down at her phone to see if they had been disconnected.

"Well, I'll be. I never thought I'd hear the word

'girlfriend' in the same sentence as either of my boys."

Alana giggled when the woman broke out in a fit of laughter. She knew that this was a desperate move, but she was a desperate woman, trying to make everything right.

"It's true. But I did something stupid, and now I've made a mess of things," she admitted.

"Honey, you sound really sweet, and the fact that you called me to help you get back with my boy tells me we're going to be really good friends. What do you need from me, darlin'?"

Alana's shoulders slumped in relief. She didn't know what to expect when she had dialed the number, but someone upstairs was truly looking out for her.

There was no way she wouldn't win back London's heart.

London stood in his family room, staring down at the items in front of him. They were the perfect, most thoughtful gifts he had ever received.

He'd been shocked when he had first received the package, knowing that he hadn't ordered anything. But to his surprise, he was rendered speechless. A three-speed stereo turntable with two built-in stereo speakers were nestled inside the box, along with an album.

That had been two weeks ago.

He picked up the album and stared at it. It was

in pristine condition. The deep blue of the background, and the man sitting on the bench next to a full moon artwork, took him back to his childhood. This album had gotten plenty of play time on Saturday mornings when his mother cleaned.

"What You Won't Do for Love," by Bobby Caldwell.

London chuckled at the memory of his mother dancing around while she folded laundry. With two growing boys who were into sports, and everything to do with the outdoors, there was always plenty of clothes that needed to be washed and put away.

London's chest tightened at the thought of how deep this gift was. Alana had truly listened to him when he spoke of his childhood. His parents both loved music, and that love had passed down to he and his brother. Neither of them could play a tune, but there were plenty of memories of them sitting around with their parents while they played their favorite tunes.

Never had he met a woman who made him feel the way she did. He could just be himself around her. She didn't care about his money or the fame. She never asked for anything from him.

He had enough money to purchase anything he wanted, but this gift was straight from the heart.

It pained him that she had thought so little of him and their budding relationship. He knew he had a track record, but the difference between the women in the past and Alana was that he truly wanted to be with her. The others meant nothing. They were a night of fun and that was it. No attachments.

He hadn't thought of another woman since he first kissed Alana. It was like something inside of him knew she was the one for him.

She was a good girl, and kept him grounded. Now that he thought about it, he could see how he was spiraling out of control. Had it not been for Alana, he would still be out there partying and hooking up with random women.

Alana made him see what was important in life. He wanted to explore the thought of a future with her.

Even now, just thinking of another woman, made him sick to his stomach.

His missed Alana's quirkiness, her big glasses, her radiant smile, and the feeling of her curves pressed against him while she slept.

Receiving her gifts, with the small note written in script, touched his soul.

Please forgive me.

London didn't know what these emotions were swirling inside of him, but he knew one thing, and that was he needed her.

A second album had been delivered yesterday. He was dumbstruck when he saw which one it was.

Coat Of Many Colors by Dolly Parton.

How the hell did she know about this one? His mother played this album until it became warped and the songs would skip. He smiled, remembering his mother screaming for him to go find a quarter to set on top of the needle to weigh it down.

It was his mother who taught him how to two-step and dance.

Making his decision, he gently placed the record on the turntable, tapped the button, and the black disk began to spin. He lifted the needle and gently placed it down onto the record.

He took a step back, his heart pounding. The music began to play, and a calming feeling came over him.

He walked over to the bar and poured himself a drink as the smooth voice of Ms. Parton floated out of the speakers.

Alana would love this. Even in this digital age they lived in, she still had her own record player.

How did someone like her practically fall into his lap? He wished she was here with him to enjoy this.

Settling on the couch, he took a sip of the fine bourbon, losing himself in the fantasy of Alana walking through the door, with a little version of him trailing behind her. She'd dance around with their son, filling the room with their laughter.

That was what he wanted.

A family. A home full of love and laughter.

With Alana.

Another week had passed, and London could admit he was no longer angry at the situation. He had felt everything from rage, anger, disappointment, and hurt. She was the one person he had given his all to, and it was like a knife to the heart to realize she hadn't believed he was true to her.

Glancing down at the latest package that had been delivered, he felt a sense of excitement.

Which album would she send?

He felt like a kid on Christmas morning, waiting to open his first gift. How had she known about the ones she had already sent? It was as if she had been granted access to his childhood bedroom, where all of his old CDs and records were.

How had he forgotten this side of himself?

He blinked.

That was easy. He had been hustling, building his empire, giving him no time for anything enjoyable. The clubs, parties, and fancy dinners weren't for him. Those were business ventures to wine and dine his clients. Countless late nights working with people in different time zones. Flying all over the country, the world, all in the name of setting up Primetime to be the best sports agency in the world.

He had taken no time to remember the things he loved as a kid.

He ripped open the package while walking through the house. Entering into the family room, he headed over to his growing collection of records and inhaled sharply at the masterpiece in his hand.

Ready to Die, by the Notorious BIG.

Seriously, how did this woman know?

This woman loved him.

There was no doubt in his mind. These gifts were chosen out of love.

He sat on the edge of the couch and pulled his phone from his pocket after placing the album next to him. Kicking off his shoes, he settled back against the pillows.

He slid his finger along the glass screen and pulled up her number.

He stared at it, hesitating.

Could they just pick up where they left off? He thought long and hard before concluding that they could. He had to take some fault in the matter for not sharing with her that he and Jaxon were twins. He only ever referred to Jaxson as his little brother. Eventually, they would have met and she would've found out. The subject just never came up.

The doorbell rang.

"Who the hell is that?" He had just gotten home from work and wasn't expecting company. Getting to his feet, he made his way into the hall and headed for the entrance.

He arrived at the large double doors, and through the glass, his gaze landed on the figure waiting for him.

London's heart raced. Quickening his pace, he threw open the door.

Alana stood there, holding a container in one hand, and a few grocery bags in the other. Wide leopard print glasses were balanced on the edge of her nose. Her hair was slicked back into a ponytail.

She was dressed in black leather leggings, a white graphic T-shirt, and leopard Chuck Taylor tennis shoes that matched her glasses.

Staring at him with wide eyes, she said, "Hi."

"Hey." He drank her in, memorizing every feature. It had been a while. He had forced himself not to go to the apartment building, knowing it would be torture for him to see her.

But now, standing in the flesh before him, he realized how much he'd truly missed her.

How much he loved her.

"I was cooking, and got a little carried away. I had a taste for chicken carbonara, made way too much for just myself, and was wondering if you were hungry?"

He watched as she took a deep breath and held it.

He stepped aside. "Come in." Releasing a breath, she slid past him, giving him a shy look. The scent of the delicious food filled his nose. Closing the door, he followed behind her as she walked into the kitchen. "Let me grab those bags."

"It's fine. I've got them."

London paused in the doorway and watched her set the items on the island.

Her eyes met his, and they froze in place.

Pushing off the doorframe, he moved to stand in front of her.

Reaching out with the tip of his finger, he gently pushed her glasses up the bridge of her nose. Up close, he could make out the dark circles under her eyes. She looked as if she hadn't been sleeping well, and a twinge of guilt filled him.

Her eyes filled with tears as she whispered, "I'm sorry."

London closed his eyes and shook his head. There was nothing for her to be sorry about. He had let his emotions take control of everything. Now that they'd had some time apart, he was able to see that this wasn't all her fault.

"You don't have to be sorry, babe." Pulling her to him, she wrapped her arms around his waist, her body shaking as she sobbed.

This situation should never had gone this far. Everything between them was good, but he had let his pride get in the way of it.

London didn't know how much time had passed, but he didn't care. He had his woman back in his arms. They would overcome this.

He tipped her chin back so he could meet her gaze.

"I just assumed—"

"Shh…" Resting a finger on her lips, he gazed at down at them, wanted to taste them. But if he did, he wouldn't be able to stop. "I shouldn't have left that day. I should've stayed so we could've had a conversation like adults."

"London—"

"This time away from each other has allowed me to think," he began. "The gifts you sent mean the world to me. No one has ever done anything so thoughtful for me before."

"I'm glad you like them." She smiled, her body relaxing against him.

"For you to dig that deep and remember something we spoke about that first day made me see how much you listen to me. It made me realize how much I missed you, and how much I love you."

Alana's brown eyes grew wide as she studied him. When she didn't move, he began to grow nervous.

He had never confessed his love to anyone before.

Wasn't she supposed to say something back?

"L–London," she stuttered. "Oh my God. I love you too."

Bending his head down, he crushed his lips to hers. She slid her hands up along his chest and wrapped them around the base of his neck, holding him in place as she pressed her curvy body close.

London basked in the taste of her. It had been so long since he held her in his arms, tasted her, that he felt as if he had just been allowed back into heaven.

He never wanted to be away from her again.

Her hips rocked against his, her moans fueling the fire he had for her. His cock grew heavy, straining against his pants.

London gripped her hips and grinded against her, wanting her to feel what she did to him.

Pulling away from her, he chuckled at her whimper of protest as he bent down and scooped her up into his arms. He made his way through the house, heading straight for the master bedroom.

Food could wait.

They had a lot of making up to do.

Alana gasped as her back hit the mattress. Once London had gotten her inside the bedroom, he'd wasted no time in getting both of them naked. She leaned up on her elbows and watched him crawl over to her. Her core clenched with need. The feral look in his eyes took her breath away.

She had taken a big chance in coming here, not knowing how he had reacted to the gifts she had sent. He hadn't called her, and she hadn't been bold enough to try to call him. She had figured she would let her gifts speak for her.

Alana had been so nervous, she was nauseas. Ever since she decided she was going to fight for him, she couldn't shake the feeling.

Widening her legs to allow him to rest between them, his hardened member brushed against her slick core, eliciting a moan from her.

She had missed him so much. Her body ached for his touch.

He captured her lips again, this kiss hard and unforgiving.

The short time they had spent apart was too long.

Deepening the kiss, London pressed his tongue inside. Stroking his tongue with hers, she wrapped her arms around him, needing more. Her body was awake, and demanding he take her.

London tore his lips from hers and began blazing a trail along her jawline. Her hips rotated against his, feeling his cock brush the entrance of her lips.

She whimpered, desperate to feel him stretch her once he slid inside. His warm body pressed against hers was heaven. She loved the weight of him above her.

A gasp escaped her when he gently nipped at her neck.

"I've missed you so much, Alana." She arched her back, thrusting her breasts against him while threading her fingers through his thick hair. He moved farther down her body, stopping at her breasts. He had always made sure he paid close attention to them. Her whimpers grew into cries of ecstasy as he licked, suckled, and nibbled on her aching mounds.

"London."

Moving from her breasts, he trailed kisses down her stomach. He had never made her feel self-conscious of her soft belly. She wasn't thin by any means, but he certainly made her feel sexy and wanted.

He finally settled between her legs, and didn't waste any time in parting her labia and latching onto her clit.

"London!" This time, his name was snatched from her lungs. The sensation of his warm mouth tugging and pulling on her sensitive bud was sending her spiraling.

He increased his pace, and she could feel the tension in her body mounting.

Her hips rocked against him, wanting him to put her out of her misery. Her climax was so close. Her breaths were coming faster. Her body writhed on the bed as he continued to work her. Only London could bring forth this response from her.

He pushed his fingers deep inside of her, setting a steady rhythm, slowly fucking her with them. Her hips rose to meet his thrusts, and she cried out from the sensation of his tongue and fingers doing such wicked things to her body.

Her fingers dove into his hair, holding on to him. She would never let him go again. No matter what, London was hers.

She closed her eyes, her muscles growing tense until she detonated.

Her cries echoed through the room while her body trembled from the intense waves of pleasure rushing through her, all while London continued his sweet torture.

Finally, when she relaxed back against the mattress, he withdrew his fingers and lifted his head.

Their eyes met, and Alana knew without a doubt that she loved him.

She hadn't expected him to be the first one to drop those three little words. She had been rendered speechless. The time away from him had been pure torture. She hadn't realized how much she'd come to need him in her life.

He rose up and crawled over her. She ran her

hands along his torso and slipped one in between them, wrapping it around his hardened cock.

"Alana," he rasped, hunger burning bright for her in his eyes. She guided him to her center, wanting to torture him a little by rubbing the head of his cock against her slick folds, coating it with her moisture. His body shuddered. "Don't play with me."

She smiled, loving how he looked, as if he was about to lose it.

She wanted to see London lose control.

With one thrust, he sunk deep into her. Her smile disappeared, and a groan ripped past her lips. Her walls stretched around him with a delicious burn.

"You think you're funny," he chuckled, capturing her lips with his as he began to fuck her.

God, she had missed this man.

He released his all on her.

Cries spilled from her lips as the force of his hips sent him deeper inside. She lifted her hips to meet him, and he raised her arms up, pressing them down onto the mattress.

His feral gaze dropped to her mounds as they bounced with each thrust.

A growl tore from his throat as his movements intensified.

Nothing else existed besides the two of them. Alana lost herself to London. She turned all of her pleasure over to him, and was soon rewarded with his hands everywhere, his lips and his cock driving her to ecstasy.

With every thrust, she cried out, teetering on the edge of her climax. His grunts grew wilder.

Alana loved every moment of it.

His hands found their way between them. Parting her folds, he stroked her clit, sending her higher.

One pinch tipped her over that cliff, leaving her to fall into the waves of immense pleasure. A scream tore from her lips as she came, just as he roared through his orgasm, his hips pumping faster, filling her up with his release. His expression was one of pure bliss.

He fell forward, his body shaking from the effects of his climax, but stopped himself from crushing her.

Alana didn't care. She wanted to feel his warm, strong body on hers. Wrapping her arms around him, she brought him down fully onto her, their skin coated with a fine sheen of sweat.

She never wanted to be apart from him again.

She was in heaven. The feeling of him nestled inside of her was something she could never tire of. They fit together, as if they were made for each other.

London shook his head, his warm breath skating along her shoulder, his heart pounding a mile a minute.

"I love you, Alana Thornton."

"And I love you, London Keith."

Kissing her shoulder, London pulled out and rolled to his side. When he was settled, he pulled her to him, resting her head on his chest.

Alana was thrilled to be in his arms again. What happened between them shouldn't have happened.

Hearing he loved her was a bonus. They needed to really talk, but for right now, she was going to remain where she belonged.

In his arms.

"How did you know?"

After a few hours, when they were finally able to leave the room, they had come back down to the kitchen.

It took both of their stomachs growling to finally pull them out of bed, and Alana had heated up the dinner she'd brought over.

The woman could cook.

He took another bite of the food and groaned.

"What are you talking about?" Smiling, she crossed her legs. He had her sitting on the island while she ate, dressed in the button-down shirt he had worn to the office, and it looked damn good on her. Her skin practically glowed, and she had that well fucked look in her eyes.

"The albums. We talked about a few songs, but the ones you sent me were so…" He stopped, unable to find the words to finish his sentence.

"Well, I have to admit, I had a little help. You mentioned you wanted a turntable, and I took it from there." She shrugged. The shirt, slightly big on her, fell to the side to reveal her shoulder.

He raised his brow. "Help from who?" Jaxon hadn't mentioned anything about speaking to Alana. Who the hell would have helped her? And who would know things so personal?

"Your mother," she whispered, nudging her glasses up the bridge of her nose. He didn't know if she realized she even did it, but the move was just downright cute on her.

"My mother?" Taking a sip of his wine, he set the glass down and moved to stand in between her legs. "When did you speak with her?"

A small smile spread across her lips. "I've actually spoken with her several times."

"Seriously?" He snagged his phone off the counter. It was late, but he didn't care.

"Who are you calling?" she asked, laughing.

Ignoring her, he pulled up his mother's number, hit send, and waited as it rang. He slid Alana to the edge, wanting to feel her body against hers. She playfully wrapped her legs around his waist. He growled and dropped a kiss to her lips.

"London Keith, do you know what time it is?" He looked at his mother's face as it popped up on the screen. He was instantly hit with a wave of homesickness, looking at the same familiar eyes he and his brother shared. He knew she was in bed, because he could see the headboard behind her. Knowing his mother, she was probably reading one of her books with a shirtless man on the cover while his father slept.

"Is that how you greet your oldest child?" he questioned. Alana watched him with a playful glint in her eyes. They had finished off the bottle of wine, with his little hellcat drinking most of it. She was tipsy, and it was adorable.

"Boy, what do you want?" Donna Keith demanded. She grinned, and it was apparent she was keeping a secret, something she was horrible at.

"It would seem you've been conspiring against me." He was trying to keep a straight face as his mother played innocent.

"Define 'conspiring.'" London could hear his father muttering in the background. "Go back to sleep, Larry. It's London," she snapped at him.

"Mom." London leveled his stern gaze at her, causing her to giggle.

"Okay. What am I supposed to do when a sweet young woman calls me asking for help to win my son back? Of course I helped the poor child out."

Grinning, London turned so that Donna could see Alana on the screen.

"Mother, I would like for you to meet Alana." He brought Alana flush against him.

"Hi, Mrs. Keith. It's nice to put a face to a familiar voice," Alana said, giving a little wave. "I can't wait to meet you in person so I can hug you."

"London, she's beautiful!" Donna gushed. "When are you bringing her home to meet us?"

London glanced at Alana before turning back to the phone.

"Really soon, Ma."

Donna's squeal filled the air.

"What the hell is going on?" Larry grumbled.

"Go back to sleep, Larry," his mother groused. She rolled her eyes and turned back to the phone. "Don't wait too long, London."

"I promise. I have a couple of important things coming up, but when I'm finished, we'll come for a visit."

He pressed a kiss to Alana's lips. His mother's squeal in the background had Alana and London falling into a fit of laughter. His mother had been on him and Jaxon about settling down, and it would seem she was about to get her wish with one of her sons.

"All right, Mom. We have to go. Love you."

"Bye, Mrs. Keith!"

"Oh, honey. There will be no more Mrs. Keith. You call me Donna."

"Okay. Talk with you soon, Donna," she replied, her words slightly slurred as she wrapped her arms around London's neck.

London disconnected the phone and set it down on the counter before taking Alana's lips in a deep, passionate kiss. He made quick work of removing her shirt, leaving her naked and just where he wanted her.

"London," she gasped when he broke the kiss to guide her down onto her back. He pushed her thighs apart, presenting her core to him. His cock was hard as steel, and pressing against his cotton shorts. The sight of Alana spread out before him on his kitchen island was an image he would never forget.

His mouth watered at the little pink pearl peeking out from Alana's brown labia. His hands ran along her slit before he dipped a finger into her silky wet heat.

London groaned at how wet she was.

"We have a lot of making up to do," he whispered.

It was the truth.

He covered her pussy with his mouth, intent on showing her how much he missed her.

"Oh, God," Alana groaned, sitting back on the floor. She barely had the strength to raise her arm to flush the toilet.

She didn't know what was wrong with her. She just couldn't shake this stomach bug. With a sigh, she closed her eyes and leaned forward, toggling the handle to flush it.

It took everything she had to stand up. Moving over to the sink, she reached for the mouthwash and gargled until the foul taste was gone.

Looking at her reflection in the mirror, she gasped.

She looked like death warmed over.

Since the day she had showed up at London's home, she had moved in. They were making plans to sell her condo. They had decided that night they no longer wanted to live apart. The commute to downtown wasn't bad.

She would miss the little shops and the neighborhood, but it wasn't the end of the world. They could always drive in and spend the day visiting all of her favorite spots.

She left out the room and snagged her cotton robe and put it on.

Today was a big day for London and Khalil. It was signing day. Khalil was officially becoming a member of the Cleveland basketball team.

Since she didn't feel well, she would support her man from home and watch it on TV. Every major media outlet would be covering it.

Alana made her way downstairs and headed to the kitchen, intent on making herself some tea. Maybe that would help her feel better. Turning on the Keurig, she went in search of a mug.

The doorbell rang.

Placing the mug on the counter, she muttered, "Who is that?" Tightening the ties of her robe, she made her way to the front door. When she stepped into the foyer, she could see Sofie standing outside the glass.

Alana swung the door open. "Hey, girlfriend."

"Damn, you are sick," Sofie huffed.

"Ha-ha." She moved to the side to allow Sofie to enter. "I shouldn't even let you in."

"Oh, you love me. You know I will always tell you the truth." Sofie brushed past her, carrying a grocery bag.

The savory scent of hot food wafted from the bag, making her feel suddenly ravenous.

"What is that?" she asked, shutting and locking the door.

"Where is the kitchen again? I swear this house is massive," Sofie chuckled.

"Follow me." Alana headed back in the direction she had just come from. Over her shoulder, she surmised, "And because you brought something that smells so good, I'll forgive your little comment."

"Since you said you weren't feeling good, I stopped and got you some soup and bread."

They arrived in the kitchen, and Alana tried to avoid looking at the island. She could feel her cheeks warm. It was one of London's favorite places to taste her.

Sofie sat her bag down on the edge of it, and Alana had to bite back a giggle. She didn't want her friend to see her; otherwise, she'd had to spill what was so funny.

She moved back to the Keurig and put her cup under it.

"I'm making some tea. You want something to drink?"

"Not tea. What else do you have?" Sofie moved over to the fridge and opened it, but Alana barely heard her. She blinked, her gaze focused on the small box sitting on the counter next to the soup.

"What is that?"

With a pop can in her hand, Sofie rolled her eyes, cracked it open, and took a hefty sip before snagging the box and tossing it to Alana.

"You need to take this," Sofie ordered.

"What? Why? I'm sick, Sofie, that's it." Even to her own ears, her words sounded hollow.

Could she be pregnant?

She knew that having sex meant there was a chance.

And with the amount of sex she and London had been having over the past few months, there was an increased possibility.

The man could barely keep his hands, tongue, mouth, and dick away from her.

Not that she was complaining. She was always ready for his advances. And hell, she didn't wait for him to make the first move.

The old Alana would never.

But with a man like London, she couldn't help it.

It was almost instinctive, and the orgasms were addictive.

But a baby?

"Don't be hesitating," Sofie said, her words breaking through Alana's thoughts. "Go. Take it right now. If you're not, then yeah, you're just sick." Her friend shrugged, as if it were a no-brainer.

But this was a big deal.

Had she and London created a life?

Nodding, Alana left the kitchen and scurried to the half bath down the hall. Shutting the door, she stood in front of the mirror, turned to the side, and opened her robe to look at her pudgy belly. It appeared to be plumper, but she assumed it was her cooking. London loved to eat, so she had been cooking way more than when she lived alone. She didn't know how he ate so much and still had the perfect muscular body.

She tried to imagine what she would look like with a basketball of a belly and grinned. She grew excited.

What if there was life growing inside of her?

Would it be a little boy with a tan who looked exactly like his father? Or a little brown-skinned girl, an exact replica of her mother?

Alana couldn't contain her excitement.

"Okay, let's do this." Within minutes, she was leaning back against the wall, waiting, the test sitting on the counter. Her heart was racing. She could barely hear anything over the pounding of it.

The instructions had said to wait three minutes before reading the results. This had to be the longest three minutes ever.

Her first instinct was to call London, but he was busy right now, and she didn't want to interrupt him or be a distraction. He would be home later.

Alana glanced at her watch.

It was time.

Stepping forward, she picked up the pregnancy test and froze.

London let himself into the house and paused. It was silent. He wasn't sure if Alana was asleep yet or not.

Today had been one of the biggest moments in his career. He had wished to have Alana there with him, but she wasn't feeling well. Her health was more important to him than any paycheck.

Khalil was now an official member of the Cleveland basketball organization. The signing bonus for London's company was massive. His sports agency was now a powerhouse for recruiting talent. They were making moves, and because of his negotiation for Khalil, he had a few other high-profile clients calling him.

But now, he wanted to have a private celebration with his woman.

He stopped at the stairs, noticing that the light from the family room was on.

She must have been waiting up for him.

He patted his inner jacket pocket, feeling the small square box resting inside. He took a deep breath and walked toward the room in search of the woman who had changed his life.

He found her curled up on the couch, snuggled underneath a blanket, with her face buried in a book. She and his mother had grown close in a short time. They spoke on the phone daily, and his mother had even gotten her hooked on her romance books.

"Hey, I didn't hear you come in." Closing the book, she sat up on the couch. He walked in and took a seat next to her. "I was watching on television. I'm sorry I couldn't be there."

"Don't worry, baby. How are you feeling?" he asked, his chest tight. He had rehearsed everything he wanted to say to her, but right now, his mind was failing him.

He wiped his hands on his pants and took her in. She was the most beautiful woman in the world to him. She was funny, intelligent, and everything about her made him want to be a better man.

For her.

"I'm good. Sofie stopped by and brought me some soup. It helped settle my stomach." She grew sheepish and tossed the book onto the table next to the couch. "But I want to hear all about it. I'm sure there were tons of people there. I kept flipping through all the channels, trying to catch different versions. Was Jaxon there?"

He laughed. She was definitely feeling better. Her inquisitive nature was so damn cute. Half the time, she didn't realize she was doing it. Questions would just flow from her lips. Her eyes would grow wide, and she'd get herself worked up from the excitement.

"I have plenty of pictures. And yes, Jax was there. It was amazing."

"I'm so proud of you."

His heart skipped a beat, and he knew this would be the perfect time. They were to go visit his parents next week, and he wanted to introduce Alana properly to his folks.

"Thanks, babe. That means the world to me," he murmured. Not wanting to wait another moment, he slid to the floor and got down on one knee before her.

"What are you doing?" She sat up straighter on the couch, her eyes locked on him. "Oh my God."

He pulled out the black velvet box holding the ring he had purchased a week ago, trying to figure out how to pop the question.

"Alana Nicole Thornton," he began, swallowing hard past the lump in his throat. So many emotions were swirling around in his chest. Opening the box, he showed her the beautiful ring he had chosen for her. The cost had not even been an option. He wanted something as close to perfect for her, and he'd finally found it. "Will you marry me?"

She blinked several times and slid to the edge of the couch, pushing the blankets to the side. A soft smile came to her lips.

"London, I… I have to share something with you."

He froze. Was she about to reject him? The thought hadn't even crossed his mind that she might. Everything was going so well between them.

"What is it, babe?"

Undoing her robe, she opened it, showing off a lace bralette and boy shorts. His eyes took her in hungrily. She looked perfect to him. He watched her hand slide to her stomach and stay there.

"I figured out why I've been so sick." Her grin widened. "I'm pregnant."

His mouth fell open. He couldn't contain the joy that filled him.

"And yes! Yes, I'll marry you!" she cried out.

Grabbing her, he picked her up and twirled her around. He couldn't believe it. Not only was the woman of his dreams agreeing to be his wife, but they were having a baby.

Setting her down, he captured her lips.

Breaking away, she danced in place and held out her hand. "Put it on me." Tears ran down her face, and London had to blink back his own, unable to believe it.

His hand shook as he pulled the ring out of the box and slid it onto her finger, which fit perfectly. He gathered her to him and sprinkled kisses along her forehead.

"Baby, I love you so much," he said, tipping her face up to his.

"I love you so much, London."

"How? When?" Dropping his hand down to her stomach, he ran it along the soft curve of her belly.

"I think it was that first weekend you brought me here." Laughing, she brought his head down and pressed her lips to his, and he immediately dominated the kiss, allowing all the emotions he felt for her to flow into it.

He tore his mouth from hers and stared down at her stomach in amazement. His child was growing inside of her.

"How?" He blinked and glanced back up at her. She wiped the trail of tears from her cheeks and barked out a laugh.

"Do you need a reminder of how to make a baby?"

London grinned at her, his cock already hard

for her. The sight of her in her barely there attire had him stiff as a board.

"Yeah, baby. I'd like that." His voice grew husky as he slid his jacket off and tossed it onto the nearest chair, then unbuttoned his shirt.

She stalked forward, forcing him to walk backward. With a little push, he fell back and down onto the couch. Her robe slid off her shoulders and floated down to the floor. Then she removed her bra and shorts.

London's mouth grew dry at the sight of his woman—his future wife—standing before him in nothing.

Alana knelt on the floor before him and reached for his belt.

When her brown eyes met his, he was a goner.

This woman was his everything, and she had just agreed to spend the rest of her life with him.

Alana made quick work of getting him out of his pants. Her lips wrapped around his cock and his head fell back.

He bit back a groan and allowed his fiancée to have her wicked way with him.

One Year Later

"What's wrong with you?" Alana spun around to see Sofie storming into the kitchen, pissed.

Time had flown by. Alana couldn't believe it had been a year since London had proposed to her. They hadn't wasted time in throwing together a small wedding with close family and friends.

Today, they were grilling out, and invited Jaxon and Sofie over to watch Khalil and his team play.

They were in the finals, and it was exciting. The game was in Los Angeles, and they opted to stay home. They had been to all the games in Cleveland. The next two games would be in town. If Cleveland won tonight's game, and the next, they would win the championship.

"What is it now?" Alana rolled her eyes and moved to the fridge to pull out the potato salad she had made and set it on the counter.

"He won't let me hold the baby. He said it's not my turn." Sofie leaned against the counter and folded her arms in front of her. If it were possible, daggers would be shooting out of her eyes.

Alana laughed. She couldn't help it. Anyone with eyes could see the sexual tension between Jaxon and Sofie. They hated each other, yet they couldn't stop eye fucking each other.

"Y'all just need to get it over with," Alana murmured. Pulling a serving spoon out of the drawer, she paused to stare at her sputtering friend.

"You think I should sleep with him? He's an arrogant ass who thinks he's God's gift to women. I refuse to be another notch on his belt."

"I'm sure a woman like you could tame him." Alana loved her brother-in-law. He and Sofie were Chance's godparents. Her son was six months old, and already had them wrapped around his little finger. Jaxon and Sofie were butting heads constantly, and it was only a matter of time until that sexual tension exploded.

She couldn't wait for that moment.

It was going to be hilarious.

"I don't think there's any cure for that man," Sofie huffed, her eyes drifting back toward the patio where Jaxon sat at the table with Chance secured to his chest. The doting uncle was obviously smitten with his nephew.

"Let's eat. The game is coming on soon, and London isn't going to want to miss it."

Everything had been perfect. She had met and fell in love with London's parents, and she and his mother were now really good friends. They were coming up in a couple of days so they could spend some time with their grandson.

"What else do you need carried outside?" Sofie asked.

"Grab a couple more beers for the guys."

They headed back outside, where London and Jaxon were deep in conversation. Their company had grown. With London's income, and the arrival of the baby, she had put in notice at her job that she wouldn't be returning after the birth of her child, opting to stay at home. It was the best decision she could have made.

She was in the midst of getting her own consulting business off the ground. She'd be able to work for herself at home, and have all the time she wanted with her family.

Alana set the salad on the table with the other items before taking the seat next to her husband.

"Hey, baby." Taking her hand, he pressed a kiss to the back of it. He had on dark aviator glasses, and she couldn't see his eyes. The man still made her heart flutter with one touch.

"Hey."

Sofie sat back, sipping on her drink. "Alana, remember our nickname for London?"

Alana's head whipped around to her friend, her eyes wide in disbelief.

Had her friend lost her marbles?

"Nickname?" London's eyebrows rose to his hairline as he squeezed her hand. "This, I've got to hear."

"I'm sure you don't want to hear it." She chuckled and turned back to Sofie, trying to give her a death glare. But apparently, her friend didn't see it, or chose to ignore it.

"Oh, please. It was funny." Sofie laughed,

tossing Alana a wink. "She would call you Mr. Hotness."

Alana covered her face as they all burst out laughing. She glanced over at London who pushed his glasses to the top of his head.

Snagging her hand, he tugged her over to him. She sat down on his lap and tried to bury her face into the crook of his neck, but he wouldn't let her.

"Really, babe? You thought I was hot?" he snickered. She rolled her eyes. Like her husband needed anything else to swell his ego. "Wait. Was the first time we met an act?"

"No. That was real!" She thought back to the day he'd opened his door and caught her about to fall over from a muscle cramp.

"That's hilarious," Jaxon said. Chance lifted his head, filled with dark, curly hair, up to look at his uncle. Jaxon ran a hand along the baby's back and grinned. "I wonder what nickname they had for me."

Reaching for her son, Jaxon handed him over to her. She wanted to cuddle her little baby boy in her arms. She looked down into the same color eyes as his father. He was going to be a little heartbreaker.

London's arms tightened around them. She

pressed a kiss to London's lips, trying to ignore Jaxon and Sofie's bickering.

"I love you."

"I love you too." He smiled at her before glancing down at Chance. "Both of you." He ran his hand along Chance's hair, making our son squeal and laugh. He was such a delightful baby, who never gave them any trouble. Alana's heart was full of love for her husband and child. She couldn't wait to see what the future held for the Keith family.

"Why do you think we would've had a nickname for you? We didn't know anything about you," Sofie snapped.

"But now? I'm sure you have one for me now." Jaxon was goading Sofie, and she was falling for it.

"Should we leave them alone?" London murmured softly against her shoulder. Alana shrugged, but couldn't take her eyes off the scene playing out before her. It was fascinating to see her friend get so riled up with Jaxon.

Yeah, the two of them just needed to get it over with and battle things out between the sheets.

"Fine. You want a nickname so bad, here's one for you—*Mr. Arrogant!*"

A Note From the Author

Dear reader,

London and Alana's story has been in the making for years. I finally decided to finish it and wow…I'm left speechless. I love being a story teller and their story was so much fun to write. I hope you love them as much as I do.

As always with my books, if you love it and want more, leave a review telling me on the platform you purchased this book!

love,

Peyton Banks

About the Author

USA TODAY best selling author, Peyton Banks is the alter ego of a city girl who is a romantic at heart. Her mornings consist of coffee and daydreaming up the next steamy romance book ideas. She loves spinning romantic tales of hot alpha males and the women they love. Make sure you check her out!

Sign up for Peyton's Newsletter to find out the latest releases, giveaways and news! Click HERE to sign up or visit her website www.peytonbanks.com!

Want to know the latest about Peyton Banks? Follow her online:

Dallas

Dalton

<u>Interracial Romances (BWWM)</u>

Pieces of Me

Hard Love

Retain Me

Silent Deception

The Christmas Secret

Mr. Hotness

<u>African American Romance</u>

Breaking The Rules

<u>Mafia Romance Series</u>

Unexpected Allies (The Tokhan Bratva 1)

Unexpected Chaos (The Tokhan Bratva 2) TBD

Unexpected Hero (The Tokhan Bratva 3) TBD